The Oasis of Filth

My Chronicle of the RL2013 Outbreak

A Novel

Part Three

From Blood Reborn

Keith Soares

Bufflegoat Books

Original publication date March 22, 2014

Special thanks to Layla, Chris, Clay Adams, Susan Gd. G. Clutter, Dennis Belmont, and Katie Mooers for their edits and contributions.

Edited by Christopher Durso.

Also from Keith Soares

The Oasis of Filth

Part 1: The Oasis of Filth

Part 2: The Hopeless Pastures

Part 3: From Blood Reborn

The Fingers of the Colossus *(Ten Short Stories)*
[Forthcoming]

1

I stood on shaking legs, one hand raised toward the woman in front of me. She lifted an eyebrow. "*Hi?*" She was confused by my greeting. And she was backed by dozens of people lined up out of the room, out of the building, into the street, piling up even as Celia and I were still dragging ourselves back to life in the small clinic, somewhere on Maryland's Eastern Shore. The woman's hand rested on a pistol strapped to one hip. I knew I had to be careful, but damn I was tired. And thirsty.

Celia stepped around me, toward the stranger. "Kate?" She looked incredulous.

"Celia? Is that you?" The woman, Kate, looked even more confused. "Wow. I only barely recognize you without... *hair*.", Kate seemed a little embarrassed for bringing that up. Celia self-consciously scraped one hand over her nearly bald head with a *scritch*, gliding across a tiny stubble of black hairs growing back slowly from her brown skin.

"Yeah, I cut it." Celia shrugged.

Kate squinted at her for a moment, then seemed to move on. We were all refugees in a world of disarray. There wasn't much point in dwelling on someone else's choice of hairstyle. "It's... good to see you again. Honestly, I'm *surprised* to see you. On your own for so long, I thought you were dead." Then she looked back to me. "But I guess you haven't been completely on your own." She eyed me up and down, unable to get a read on the scraggly, pale, bloodstained old man standing in front of her. I couldn't help but laugh. Again, Kate raised an eyebrow.

Celia gave a brief — and heavily edited — description of how and why she came to be traveling with me. She left out the real reason she had separated from the refugee group that had left Norfolk. But she did mention Addy. She paused, conflicted between feelings of love, anger, and betrayal. The dog had nearly killed her.

"We saw all the blood back in the fields," Kate said with a solemn look. She pointed at me. "You're saying he brought you back from *that*?" Now she was beyond confused.

"I used to be a doctor," I said. "In another life. Time immemorial. But I guess I remember some things." I scratched at my scruffy face absently.

Kate stared at me in an all-too-familiar, almost greedy way. Back when I lived within the walls of DC, I used to see that same look on the people in line with me at the old Capitol Hill Community Food Dispersal Center. A desire to have what someone else had. Then, it was food. For Kate, it seemed it was me. A doctor. It gave me pause. I didn't like Kate thinking of me as a commodity, especially one she coveted. I grimaced and turned away.

"Seems like everybody thinks *doctor* is a magic word," I said. I raised my voice and scanned the eyes of everyone crowded into the room, then looked back to Kate. "It isn't. These days, with no medicine or fancy equipment, I can do something when there are broken arms to set, or wounds to clean and stitch. But infection and disease? I'm as lost as you. I might be able to tell you *what* you have, but without medicines, all I can tell you is how soon you'll die."

Kate lowered her chin, her hand finally moving off her pistol. In her stained green shirt and jeans, she looked weathered, imposing. I realized then that she wasn't just the person who happened upon us, she was this group's leader. She scratched behind one ear, then spoke.

"We have two nurses with us. They're good. But your training… it may give us more options."

May? Well, I guess these days that was about right. At least that look of near-lust was off her face.

"What're you saying?" Celia asked.

Kate turned to her. "Join us." Celia hesitated, even taking a half step backward. Kate continued. "I assume you're thinking about Burt. I don't know what he did to you, Celia, but I know what you did to him, and I know what he was like. Whatever that bastard did, it had to have been something bad to make you take his eye." Celia's face was stone, but Kate didn't flinch. "And to make you kill him." Celia opened her mouth, closed it. Kate wore the look of someone who was used to knowing more than everyone else. "Aaron told us you shot Burt. At that house by the bay, where you two must've lived." Aaron must be the skinny sidekick, the one who got away.

I frowned at Kate. It had been a long time since anyone knew much of anything about me, and I didn't like hearing her tell a story that I knew firsthand and she knew third. I started to say so when Aaron himself burst into the clinic.

Tall and gangly, with the same stringy, unkempt blond hair he'd worn when he and Burt arrived at the cabin, Aaron looked at us with something like shock. Then he saw Kate standing across the room. "Oh my God. Celia. Well, isn't this nice?" Aaron's tone was mocking. He puffed himself up, seeming to expect the group to support him. "Kate knows about you, Celia. She knows all about what you did, and you're gonna pay for it."

"I'll pay?" Celia frothed. "*I'll pay?* What crime did *I* commit, Aaron? The crime of being raped by Burt, with your help? Or maybe you mean that I killed Burt. The man who *raped* a member of the group, just because he was in charge." Kate and the others pressed closer, hands on their weapons, and I reached out for Celia, trying to calm her. She brushed me aside.

Aaron looked at Celia with disdain. "Rape?" he asked. "Is that what you're calling it now?"

Celia seethed, fisted clenched. I knew her too well. *Don't*, I thought. *Don't.* She did. Spying the medical supplies on a nearby counter, Celia snatched up a pair of scissors and raged toward Aaron.

He raised his pistol from its holster, and she stopped, frozen.

Aaron was smug. "You see, Kate, dontcha? She's not right. She's violent. Just like I told you. Maybe she's *infected*, you know?" He smiled, then went straight-faced, an awful attempt to hide his true feelings. "You best drop that, Celia," he said, and she complied, tossing the scissors back on to the counter with a *clang*. Everyone's eyes went to Kate.

I saw that she had quietly trained her pistol on Aaron, holding it low, at her waist. After a pause, he noticed it, too, and Kate spoke. "Aaron, your true intentions are no mystery. And Burt wasn't what I'd call an innocent victim. Put the gun *down*."

Aaron withered. His gun slid sideways and ended up pointing at Kate, perhaps inadvertently, but she didn't miss the gesture.

Several others saw what was happening and turned their guns on Aaron, too. Even he could see that he was hopelessly outmatched. He might have killed Kate with a quick shot, but his victory would be short-lived. He nervously looked around at the weapons facing him.

"Hey, now," he said, licking his lips. "What's this?" His eyes roamed the room, but his pistol remained on Kate.

Her voice was brutally serious. "You will point your weapon somewhere else if you know what's good for you, Aaron." Her tone was unmistakable. One false move and he would die. Suddenly, I liked the idea of Kate as group leader.

A moment passed and no one gave in. I steeled myself for the ensuing gunfire, stepping instinctively to block Celia from harm.

After just bringing her back from the dead, I'd be damned if was going to let someone gun her down.

Then Aaron dropped his gun, returned it to its holster. "Kate. Seriously?" He was indignant now, trying to hide his sheepishness. "You're not turning this back on *me*, are you? This woman *killed* one of *us*."

Kate paused. But her resolve didn't swerve. "She killed a man that probably deserved every inch of killing he got." Aaron knew he had lost not only the battle but the war, and gears seemed to be turning in his head, trying to figure out what to do next. Kate lowered her pistol, but no one else in her group did. Apparently they took any threat to their leader very seriously. Celia and I remained frozen, unwilling to enter into this internal struggle.

Kate turned away from Aaron, now ignoring him. "I apologize for the interruption," she said, calmly returning her gaze to Celia and me. Behind her, Aaron fumed. Even more than her words or her gun, Kate's *dismissal* clearly stung him. He turned and stormed out of the room, pushing past people angrily, and several gun barrels followed him until he was gone. Kate looked at each of us. "We could use a doctor. Will you join us?"

She was all business. I wondered if Celia took offense that Kate's offer didn't really mention her at all, or what she might bring to the table. And I loathed that a tiny part of me was relishing the attention of once again being important. I scowled. "Yeah, we'll join you. For a while."

"*What?*" Celia wheeled to face me, incredulous. I met her gaze, trying to calm her without words.

"But no commitments," I quickly added, addressing Kate, but looking into Celia's eyes, hoping she'd understand. "No expectations. I'm not a miracle machine."

Kate looked skeptical. She glanced down at Celia's patched leg, and I could tell she thought otherwise. Her eyes met mine. "Deal." She held out a hand. "Can you travel?"

"I think so." I took her hand and we shook on it, as if that meant anything anymore. But it felt appropriate.

Celia stayed quiet, brow furrowed, her eyes boring holes through me.

2

"Are you *crazy*?" Celia asked in a hushed tone after most of the group had left the clinic.

I stopped packing our meager gear. "Maybe. But what good is it going alone now? There's strength in numbers." What a hackneyed phrase. Celia's grimace told me she wasn't buying it.

"And danger, too," she hissed back. "What about *Aaron*...?" I knew that Aaron wouldn't be the only bad seed in such a large group. I just hoped that with a leader like Kate, most everyone else would be good people. Or at least stay in line. My recent experience with human nature told me I'd be very lucky for that to be the case.

I pulled a bottle of water from one of our packs and took a huge drink, and thought for a moment. "You recognized her," I said. "What do you know about Kate?"

"She was with us. After we got out of Norfolk. After the tunnel." Celia shuddered at the memory of her long, dark flight from a known enemy and into an unknown world. "Burt — the guy I killed back at the house — was pretty much in charge, and Aaron was with him, but mostly because no one else stepped up."

"They were in charge, but you told me you didn't know Aaron's name. How's that?"

She chuckled, but there was no humor in her voice. "We called him *Ernie*, because he and Burt were inseparable. But I knew that wasn't his real name. Anyway, I think a lot of people could see Kate would be better for the group, me included. So at least I can say that I think the group's better now, with Kate in charge."

Okay, that was a good start. Celia confirmed some of my impression of Kate. Maybe we could work it out.

I still felt obligated. Now that I knew it was *possible*, I had to figure out a way to help them, help someone, overcome the disease. "Do you know where they're headed?" I asked. "Are they looking for The Oasis?"

"Probably," Celia said. "There were a lot of different rumors when we were traveling."

"Why north?"

"Baltimore was one possibility. So was Syracuse, up in New York. But they may be headed somewhere else."

I considered the long, cold march to upstate New York, and knew I had to stop this mad rush to nowhere.

My blood had saved Celia. But I couldn't start giving out transfusions to everyone in the whole group. Not without dying. And, for the first time in a long time, I felt like there was a *reason* not to die. I felt like there was something I had to do.

But *how?*

Damn it, I wished Rosa was there. I was a general practitioner, a family doctor, meaning I knew enough to be dangerous. She was the medical research specialist. I *needed* her. The thought made me wince. And Celia noticed.

"What?" she asked. She was frozen, studying me.

I felt like I'd been caught. "Nothing," I said, turning away.

Celia rolled her eyes. "Listen. I get it. You lost someone really, really special to you. I lost my brother, my parents, friends, and... Addy, too." The memory was bittersweet for both of us. "Everyone's lost someone special. Someone that *should* have been with them to the end. But you've got to get it together. We need to be smart."

I scoffed. Really? Celia, basically a child, was going to lecture me on what I needed to do. That I needed to get it together? It made me angry. I considered a really ugly remark or two, but instead I waited. I was too old for that sort of nonsense. I took a breath.

"Celia. You're right. And you're wrong. It's true, I was thinking of Rosa. But not just in some wistful way. Hell, that's a disservice to her memory anyway. She was better than that. You know, she didn't *find* the cure to the disease, but she was the one who found the way to spread it. Now it looks like *I'm* the damn cure. And I don't know how to spread it. The only thing I can figure is that we need to connect with people — maybe a *lot* more people — until we see who can help us figure this out. If Rosa was here, I bet she'd know. But she's not. So we need to find others. And that's why we need this group." Celia seemed to thaw a little. I pressed on. "And besides, I'm tired. I don't know if I can keep trying on my own. Or even just the two of us. I'm a lot older than you, remember?"

She lowered her chin and gave me a wry look. "Did you think I could forget *that?*"

"Okay, smart aleck. Are we agreed? We join the group?" I lifted our near-empty bag of provisions.

The gesture wasn't lost on her. We had nothing else. "Yeah, come on," Celia said, and walked past me and out of the room.

* * *

Outside, we noticed the chill in the air as we caught up with Kate, but the late fall scent of decaying leaves decay conjured up pleasant memories, not bad ones. Sunday-afternoon football and trick-or-treating and a thousand other things we might never do again. Kate sat on a bench outside the caved-in remains of a bike shop, examining some items that members of the group had found in the small town — cans of food, a couple bottles of water, and several winter coats. Seeing the coats made me feel the cold wind even more. If we didn't find a more permanent home, we were all going to need a lot more than those few coats very soon.

"Where're you headed?" I asked Kate bluntly as we stopped in front of her.

She paused, looked up. From her eyes, I sensed that she was silently asking herself and me why she needed to justify her actions to a new person, an outsider, a no one. But she waved away the others who were gathered loosely around her, so that only she, Celia, and I stood together.

"Baltimore, most likely. At least, that's the current plan."

I frowned. "*Baltimore*? Why?"

Kate blinked. She wasn't used to being second-guessed. She paused, gauging her answer. I knew right then what the truth was. No matter what she said, I'd made up my mind. She was hoping The Oasis was in Baltimore.

But she wasn't going to admit that to us. "We discussed this as a group," she said. "Baltimore seems like a good place to find a pocket we can fortify and make our home —"

"Are you kidding?" I said. Celia shot me a warning look. *Take it easy.*

Kate was aggravated, but simply raised her eyebrows and said, "I take it you disagree."

I flailed my hands. "Baltimore fell right at the beginning. What do you think you'll find there?"

Kate didn't flinch. "Walls. Safety. Security. A place to start again."

"Walls that *fell*. Safety that was a *lie*. Security for *no one*." I stopped myself, took a breath. Changing my tone, I asked, "Have you heard something about Baltimore, something that makes you want to go there?"

Ever so slightly, Kate blushed, and she turned away. My hunch was right.

"The Oasis, *right?*" It wasn't a question so much as an accusation.

Kate froze. She wasn't used to people guessing her mind. She looked like she was fumbling for a response. "All right," she said, nodding. "I can see I'm not dealing with someone who blindly plays 'follow the leader.' The Oasis. That's it. That's what we're hoping to find." She spoke like she was daring me to argue with her. But knowing what I knew, what choice did I have? Just to follow along?

"The *Oasis?*" I didn't mean to sound derisive, but I'd been in her shoes before. I'd blindly plodded down this path, hoping The Oasis was at the end. By chance, the *true* Oasis was at the end of that one path, but I knew it wasn't at *the end of all of them*. I twisted my eyes back to meet Kate's. "Well. Just stop." I wasn't sure what to say, or how to say it. But the words came out anyway. "It's not there."

"And you know this *how?*" Kate's cold eyes studied me.

Before I fully thought about the consequences, I said, "Because it was in South Carolina. I was there." I could see she didn't quite believe me, and so, like I fool, I forged on. "They even had the cure, and they fell. There's nothing left there now."

Kate gasped.

Immediately, I realized my folly. I'd just met this woman, these people. And now, I was telling them everything. *Who cares? Shouldn't they know?* My mind was as tired of this aimlessness as my weary muscles and bones.

Kate held her tongue, like someone who was used to sizing up other people, trying to figure out whether to believe them. "You're... *serious*, aren't you?" she asked.

I grimaced. "Yeah, I am." Kate's expression didn't change, but something in her eyes collapsed, and guilt hit me. I had just taken away the one thing that gave her hope.

"Wait…" I started, then stopped, not knowing the right thing to do or say.

Kate looked into my eyes. "Tell me the whole story, everything about The Oasis, or I have no reason to believe you, and we'll head to Baltimore as planned." She was shrewd and to the point. I owed her the truth. But I had no intention of telling her anything about Rosa. No one got those memories for free. So she heard a shorter version, one that I hoped left out all the questions I didn't want her asking. I told her about leaving DC, the search, finding the camp, then the cure. And then I told her about the fall.

Kate was quiet. Seconds seemed like hours, as if I could count the span of time between her eyes blinking. Finally, she looked at me again. "You're *cured?*" she asked in a low voice.

I hesitated, suddenly aware of what my next response might mean. Still, her eyes never wavered. And, for better or worse, I relented. With a sigh, I said, "Yes."

Celia fidgeted next to me, and Kate's attention was drawn to her. "And you? Were you at The Oasis, too? Are you cured?"

"No — well, um." Celia hesitated.

Kate turned back to me. "Which is it?" she asked. coyly, regaining her normal demeanor as the head of the group.

Celia was flummoxed, not used to the scrutiny. "It's both," she said. "And neither..."

"Both yes and no," I said. "Celia wasn't *at* The Oasis. But she *is* cured. I just cured her, back where you found us."

Kate almost couldn't comprehend what I was saying. "*You cured her? Here? Now?*"

Where moments ago I had taken away Kate's hope, now I gave her something even more. She beamed a broad smile.

3

If you were living in hell, and there was news of free ice water, that news would travel fast. Not surprisingly, so did the news of the cure.

By the time our conversation with Kate was over, a knot of wide-eyed people had formed around us. They looked at Celia and me like we were saviors. Or mythic creatures. Or freaks.

It wasn't long before the murmuring began. Among the low tones, I could hear bits of questions, demands... *Give it to us ... Why are they keeping it to themselves? ... Can we take it from them?*

Kate heard these, too, and showing herself to be a true leader, she stepped up onto the bench she'd been sitting on when Celia and I had first walked up. A cool breeze brought the early, foreboding scents of winter, pushing aside the more complex aromas of fall.

Turning left and right, Kate waved her hands and shouted, commanding everyone's silence and attention. "Enough! Listen. I understand. Like you, I just found out that our new companions *may* be cured of the infection. Hell, right now, no one knows if that is even *true*, but I don't know what good it'd do to lie about it. And I'm excited. And scared. And thrilled. And thinking about a better tomorrow. But we don't know enough yet." She gestured to me to come closer. When I did, she crouched down and whispered in my ear, *"Tell us all how we can be cured."* The mix of hope and desperation in her voice was painful to hear, especially when I knew what my answer had to be.

I looked down at the cracked sidewalk, another memento from a vanished age, from a time when lovers and families strolled safely and aimlessly down the street, and I gathered my thoughts. As the wind blew colder, I turned to the group, and saw all eyes on me, nearly 200 in all. I decided to rip the bandage off first. "I can *not* cure you all!" I shouted. A collective moan emanated from the group. "At least, not immediately. Not today." In the back, where the bravest cowards always hide, there were jeers of *Why not?* and *He's lying!* Kate moved to intervene, but I waved her off. "Hold on, hold on," I said. "I understand you all want this with every fiber of your being. To be cured. To make this long nightmare end. But I can't do that for you *now*." More murmurs from the back.

"I've been to The Oasis. I've been cured of the disease. But I have to tell you that The Oasis is gone." Gasps and wails, but I pushed onward. "My friend Celia here, she was a member of your group when you left Norfolk. She and I met by chance, and later she was bitten and infected. I didn't know what to do, but I didn't want her to die, so I gave her a blood transfusion." People looked at me skeptically. "Not only did she live, she lost all signs of the disease. She was *cured*."

A renewed fervor of cries, people demanding the cure for themselves. "I used to be a doctor," I said, my voice fraying with the effort, "back before the outbreak, but that doesn't mean much anymore. But I think my blood knows how to fight the infection, and through the transfusion, Celia's blood does, too. That's the good news."

People alternately cheered and demanded more, some demanded their cure immediately. It was time to drop the hammer. "This is the bad news. Even if I wanted to cure every single one of you, right now that would mean giving you each a transfusion of my blood. Not only is that generally risky, it's not something I can physically do. Back before the outbreak, the general rule of thumb was only to give blood every eight weeks. And that was just for giving a pint of blood — I gave a lot more to Celia. It may take a lot more to make this work, I don't know. But if I have to wait eight weeks between every transfusion, and there are, what, a hundred of you all? That's a long time. And I might die doing it. Or one of you might die, from some complication."

Shouts again in the back. *Make the woman do it, too!* I couldn't blame them for wanting to be cured, but I needed to defuse a potential mob scene. In a low voice, I asked Celia, "Do you know your blood type?"

"AB, I think," she replied, unsure. I grimaced. My O type was the "universal donor," while hers was far from it. If we needed plasma, she'd be great, but in most cases my blood was the only one that was going to help.

I called back to the crowd. "Celia's blood type isn't right. If some of you remember anything about blood types — A, B, AB, O — and about donating blood, you'll know what I mean. My blood is type O, and I can give it to any of you. Celia thinks hers is AB. And that won't work."

Grumblings told me they weren't all convinced. I kept at it. "But I want you all to know this. I want to help you. I want you to have the cure. I just need your help. We need to find a way to make it possible for me to give it to you all, and to replicate what I have. That's why we want to join you, and that's why I *don't* want you all to go to Baltimore!"

Kate flinched, clearly upset at me for going to the group when our discussion hadn't been concluded. She stabbed a look of anger in my direction, then jumped up. "Okay, folks," she said, arms stretched out to her sides, hands gesturing for folks to calm down. "I know many of you want more answers, but now you know everything we know. We're here in this town, the sun won't stay out forever, and it's already getting pretty cold. We'll stay here until morning. Everyone, find shelter. Eat at daybreak, pack and out one hour after that. That's it, go about your needs." She clapped her hands, and it was clear she was dismissing the group. Some grumbling remained, but everyone listened and went about their duties.

In the back, I saw Aaron. As the others separated and moved to their various chores, he stood still, staring at me.

4

"DC," I said the next morning as Kate and her inner circle packed gear and readied to go.

"What?" she asked, annoyed.

"We need to go to DC," I said, crossing my arms, unflinching. "That's the best place to find the people and the labs where we can figure out how to spread this cure. Baltimore is just chasing ghosts."

"Well, I appreciate your unsolicited input, but we're going to Baltimore," Kate said. "This has been decided. You don't just tag along and get to call the shots." Her offhanded dismissal told me I'd better be careful. If I wanted to have a say in what the group did, where we went, I needed to start earning her trust.

"Take the Bay Bridge," I said.

Kate stopped working items into her backpack and turned to me, curious, concerned. "We thought about it," she said, "but we're concerned about being exposed, and about the condition of the bridge."

"I walked it a few months back. It was fine then, I bet it still is now." I knew the bridge was the fastest way to Baltimore, a desirable choice if that was her goal. Plus, it was the most direct route toward DC.

Kate thought about it, then seemed to come to a decision. "We'll take a look at it. I'd rather not go all the way around if we don't have to." Then she leaned in close. "But listen. You need to understand a few things. I don't make arbitrary decisions. You standing up and making me look bad doesn't help *anyone*. If people stop responding to my leadership, fine, but I don't see anyone else stepping up. Most of these people just need some sort of structure or else they'll give up. Before I took over, Burt was in charge." She paused to let that sink in. "You met Burt, albeit briefly. I'm sure you got a good sense for what kind of leader he was. People needed something more, someone better, someone they could trust. I didn't want the job, but folks wanted someone who'd help them, not bully them. I was basically drafted, and by enough people that Burt couldn't argue. Aaron has no love for me, and there are others who dissent. It happens. So when you stand up and disrespect me, rally people against me, you're helping Aaron and his kind. Is that really what you want?"

My respect for Kate grew in bounds as she spoke. Still, I had to ask. "You think every decision you make is the *right* one for the group, then?"

Kate shook her head. "Wouldn't that be nice? No, I don't. But at least I do *think*."

"Then why not listen to reason about Baltimore?"

Kate seemed ready for that. "People need hope. They believe The Oasis is in Baltimore. We *need* to go there, even if we don't find anything. Otherwise, they'll always be wondering, trying to get away to see for themselves, rather than help us here. Now."

I could hardly argue with her. Hadn't Rosa and I been drawn to The Oasis not so long ago? "Listen," I said. "I want what you want — good for the group. And more than that, I want good for *humanity*. I'm bringing you a new hope." I knew I sounded ridiculous, but kept looking at her, silently pleading, no more words to offer.

After a moment, she nodded. "If it's clear, we take the bridge. After that, we'll talk." She pointed a finger at me. "But *don't* go lobbying the group with speeches again."

I bowed my head in agreement.

* * *

It took two days to march the group to the eastern edge of the Bay Bridge, with men, women, and children hauling everything they owned on their backs, in push carts, or in wheelbarrows. The bridge was actually two different spans, one next to the other. Out of habit, we followed the backed-up line of abandoned cars until we reached the northernmost stretch, a three-lane slab of road pockmarked with ragged holes.

As the morning dragged on, the weather began deteriorating, with a slow, cold rain falling. At the foot of the bridge, Kate stopped to assess what she saw. One of her closest advisers, a tall, muscular blond kid named Jacob, handed her a pair of binoculars. She studied the bridge, or at least the part she could see in the rain. After a while, she announced her decision. "It's got plenty of defects, but it looks solid if we're careful. But I don't like this weather." As if in response, the wind kicked up. She turned to Jacob and another adviser, a sturdy, short-haired brunette named Vera. "What do you think? Bridge, or north and around?" Her gaze swept to the right, northward. The bay stretched as far as our eyes could see. I could smell the damp sweetness of rotting leaves, and tried to concentrate on nothing beyond the steady drum of the rain.

It was clear that no one wanted to take the long road. Finally, with a curt nod, Vera said, "We should take the bridge."

Kate returned the nod and it was done. We prepared to move out. "We'll take the front," Kate said. "Tell Marcos, Yolanda, and…" She considered her options. "And Aaron to take the back. Let's get going." Kate's lieutenants passed down her orders, and we began crossing the bridge, hoping the weather would hold.

It didn't.

KEITH SOARES

5

The Chesapeake Bay Bridge is more than four miles long. An average human walks at about three miles per hour, but our speed was reduced significantly by the size and makeup of our group. Adding to the problem, the bridge had countless little gaps and breaks, and, as we made our way along its convex surface, we noticed the grasses and other small plants that had been sprouting in pockets and corners where dirt had accumulated since the outbreak. It was a surreal reclamation by nature of something inherently unnatural.

As we progressed along the bridge, getting higher, I sensed a collective feeling of unease. People pulled their coats more tightly against themselves, and clustered toward the center of the road, as far from the edges as they could get. The water fell to more than a hundred feet below us, an icy grave for anyone who was careless enough to fall. It was more than two hours before we reached the halfway mark, and for most of that time we were looking back constantly to ensure the group and its provisions were still with us.

Then the weather got worse. The wind increased dramatically as the rain intensified. Our visibility was cut to 250 feet, maybe less. Kate soldiered on, trying to lead the group over the midway point, so we could start on the faster downhill side.

It was as good an idea as any. But without warning, three infected attacked the rear of the group. My guess is they'd been holed up in one of the many wrecked cars on the bridge, or maybe in several of them, and we drew them out as we passed. They launched themselves at our rearguard. Seeing them, Aaron lost what little spine he had and came running forward through the group, leaving his point unguarded. As the zombies attacked, I later learned, Marcos and Yolanda tried to repel them. But without Aaron, there was an opening.

Near Yolanda, a mother was trying to coax her tired and unwilling young son to follow the group. The boy, with a mop of dirty blond hair and an untucked plaid shirt, resisted in the way only exhausted children can, not understanding his own plight. They'd been making their way slowly across the bridge, barely keeping up. Without Aaron to stop it, one of the zombies hit the mother and son like a freight train, knocking her down and sending the boy tumbling on the wet pavement. After an initial scream of surprise, the mother saw what was happening and shrieked. The zombie mercilessly leaped onto the young boy.

From the front, we heard a gunshot rip through the air, for a moment stilling even the sound of the storm, and we all stopped. Then came the mother's horrific wail. I looked to Kate, saw her breath puff like clouds in the frosty air, the pitiless rain continuing to fall all around us. Her hair was wet, matted to her forehead, and her expression was one of determination and resignation. Without a wasted moment, she rushed through the group toward the source of the noise. Celia and I followed. Along the way, we passed Aaron, who was scrambling in the opposite direction. Kate shouted something at him that was lost in the rising sounds of the storm and the commotion.

A mother. Howling over her lost child. As if in answer, the wind began to rage and the cold rain pounded even harder, almost blinding us.

Nearing the scene, we saw mayhem and slowed to get our bearings, just for a moment. Something was happening to our right, hard to see in the rain. In the center of the bridge, Yolanda stood over a dead zombie, her gun drawn. Then we saw the mother, a petite brunette in soaked jeans and a soiled red coat, as she madly dove at the zombie that was on her son. In an instant, it turned on her. We ran to help.

Just before we reached them, Kate vanished.

Panting, I swiveled my head to look for her. I was disoriented, saw nothing in the pouring rain. My attention was drawn back to the horrible scene in front of me. I was weak from the transfusion, slower from age. I could do little but stare. The boy seemed to already be dead. The mother wasn't far behind. The zombie had knocked her down, and although she fought, it was stronger than she was. Celia ran toward them, delivering a kick to the gut of the zombie that sent it rolling off the woman. But the effort was hard on Celia and her newly repaired leg. She crumpled, landing on the road just feet from the infected monster.

Screams seemed to come from every direction around us. The rain, wind, people running everywhere, fighting. It was impossible to take it all in.

The zombie rolled, began to get up. Celia tested her leg, and, although she grunted from the pain, she stood and began backing away. The soaking wet zombie, what remained of a large man in a tattered jacket and ragged slacks, maybe a businessman or lawyer in his former life, rose up and took a step toward her. And another shot rang out. The zombie's forehead exploded, and he fell backward.

For a moment, Yolanda just stood there, shaking, her pistol held out in front of her, like her arm was frozen. A sound came from the right — a man's desperate cry. Yolanda snapped out of it, whipped around. Through the rain, we could barely make out Marcos, fighting another one of the infected.

Near the crumbling outer wall of the bridge, Marcos staggered. One zombie lay beheaded near his feet, but another had grabbed him from behind, and Marcos flailed to get it off. His weapon, a rusty but formidable-looking scythe he'd probably pillaged from some Eastern Shore barn, was useless with the zombie so close.

"*Marcos!*" Yolanda shouted. She waved her gun, but it was clear she didn't have a shot. Marcos and the zombie continued to struggle. Marcos pushed upward into the zombie's face, trying to get it off his back. The thing bit down onto his left hand, tearing through flesh, and Marcos screamed. In pain, he twisted and shoved, desperate to get free.

We saw what was happening just a moment before it was too late.

Whether Marcos intended it or not, I couldn't tell, but with a lurch they both tumbled over the edge of the bridge and were gone. Even the sound of their fall, their crash into the frigid waters below, was lost in the howling wind.

I gazed around at the others, stunned. Celia stood with her mouth agape. Yolanda slowly lowered her pistol. Some others in the group who had witnessed the fight remained cowering where they were, unbelieving. We all shivered in the cold, whimpered, traded hollow stares.

At that moment, a voice echoed in my head from a distant past. I had been in residency at a small hospital in rural Virginia, shadowing a codger named Dr. Hawthorne, when three people were rushed in. They'd been in a bad car accident. One of the three was nearly cut in half, and all I could do was stare at his lifeless form. Hawthorne leaned toward me, and in a whisper, harsh, not unkind, said, "There's nothing to be done for the dead. Save all you do for the living." Then he rushed to help the other two victims, and I followed.

Leaving my daydream, I thought of the young mother on the bridge in the cold rain, and ran to her side. Her breath was rapid, ragged, and she was soaked in icy rainwater and blood. I checked her pulse and felt nothing, not knowing how much of the problem was my fingers, numb from the cold. Nonetheless, I figured she didn't have long. I turned toward the boy and could see that the life had already left him. *There's nothing to be done for the dead.* At least neither of them would have the indignity of becoming zombies themselves. It was very small solace.

Standing, I looked toward Celia and Yolanda, and I could see the question in their eyes. I shook my head. *"Both?"* Yolanda asked, desperately. I nodded, and her shoulders fell.

That's when we heard a new sound. It was barely audible. A low, plaintive cry, coming from somewhere nearby. *"Help —"*

"Is that...?" Celia turned her head.

"Kate!" Yolanda shouted, completing Celia's thought. Instantly, we spread out, frantically looking for Kate. We swept around abandoned cars and debris, searching the width of the bridge. Others who had been huddled in fear now turned their heads, rose to their feet, tried to help us locate her.

Near the northernmost edge of the bridge, down low, I saw her hair.

Kate hung below the bridge, in a ragged crack that cut deep into the surface, her feet dangling freely some 150 feet above the cold waters of the Chesapeake. It seemed impossible. What kept her from falling? Surely she couldn't be hanging on by her own strength, not for this long. I reached down, looking for a way to help her back up without sending myself off the edge. And I discovered what had saved her. Or perhaps what had damned her.

As I reached down to help lift her back to the bridge deck, my hand scraped against a thin shaft of rusted metal — *rebar*. I saw several of the twisted bars poking out of the crumbled edge of the bridge. Three or four of them had dug into Kate's clothes, acting like an industrial-strength coat hanger. But one stabbed directly into Kate's right armpit. Blood streamed down the rebar, obscenely bright against the dull metal, and her right shoulder was hunched up at a strange angle. Kate appeared to be in shock, but still had the strength to shout in pain when I started to move her.

"Is she okay?" Celia asked, appearing next to me, Yolanda right behind her. "Is she gonna make it?"

"Only if she's lucky. But first, we have to get her out of this crack." I stood, gave Celia and Yolanda a serious look. They seemed overwhelmed by the yawning gap that opened below Kate. I needed to focus them. "It's going to hurt her," I said. "*A lot*. But if we fail, she either bleeds to death here or she falls. So when we move her, it has to be all the way up, all at once. No second chance, understand?" They nodded, gravely. "We need help, too." I looked around at the other members of the group who had joined us, pointed at a strong-looking young guy with a thick, dark beard. "*You*! We need your help here, right now!" I didn't leave room for rebuttal. He looked around, sheepishly, hoping I was pointing at someone else, but joined us.

As quickly as possible, we prepared a wheelbarrow as a makeshift gurney. Then it was one big tug, wrenching Kate up, screaming in pain, out of the crack. Slumped in the wheelbarrow, she reminded me of Celia only days before. We started to move and I did my best to plug up the wound, but I needed someplace dry to work. *Fast.*

So we rushed to the western shore ahead of the group, maneuvering around cars, dodging holes. Bumping over rubble as Kate screamed until she passed out.

The rest followed as quickly as a hundred souls —now 97 souls — could manage, hoping the bridge held no more surprises.

6

The rain had slowed to a drizzle by the time we made it to the far side of the bridge. Celia, Yolanda, and I trotted alongside of Kate in her wheelbarrow gurney. The young man with the beard — his name was Evan — pushed.

As we came off of the bridge, we saw two structures. To our left were the destroyed remains of the eastbound tollbooth. At some point, probably during the massive evacuations that accompanied the first outbreak 10 years ago, cars had taken out most of the supports, and the roof had caved in. But on our right, a red-brick building stood whole. It was marked with a faded four-color Maryland crest above its door, and just in front of the building stood a small bell. I couldn't tell for sure, but it seemed like a replica of the famous Liberty Bell from Philadelphia. The reminder of time gone by momentarily shook me. Old phrases and notions popped into my head, vestiges of an education that now felt useless. *Give me liberty or give me death!* Hell, just give me a minute to breathe. I wouldn't know what to do with liberty, and I'd had enough of death.

We entered the building, with Evan now backwards-hauling Kate up a few stairs. Thankfully, she remained unconscious, and we were glad to be out of the spitting rain. It even felt nominally warmer, since the walls cut the wind. I grabbed for my pack. As the others slid debris off a table and moved Kate onto it, she awoke, briefly. In a low, strained voice, she said, "We have supplies. Get Renee. She's a nurse. She has what you need." Then she faded out again.

I nodded at Yolanda, and she left to pass word to Renee, who was still part way up the bridge. We had to wait for her arrival.

Even unconscious, Kate seemed to moan as I pressed on her wound, desperate to slow the bleeding. Finally, Renee arrived. She wore a backpack, a dour expression shadowing her face. "You have medical supplies?" I asked. She nodded, then she looked down at Kate, lying on the table, with a sense of disdain that I didn't understand. Shaking it off, I asked for the supplies I needed, and Renee took them from her pack.

Without anesthesia, we simply plowed forward. "Do you have sutures, ski needles?"

Renee glared at me. "I know how to do my job," she said, pushing me out of the way. Still, I peered over Renee's shoulder to inspect the wound. Kate was lucky. The rebar that had gathered in her clothing was what stopped her fall. She had scratches and cuts here and there, but they were minimal, and the major injury to her right armpit was manageable. Some cleanup and a few sutures, stuff Renee could ably handle, although I watched her work carefully. Barring infection, Kate would live. Renee finished the work silently, and left.

As if on cue, Aaron stormed in. Behind him, a small group of supporters streamed through the door. "There you are!" he spat.

Yolanda reacted first, lifting her pistol. "Shut your mouth, you son of a bitch. You abandoned your post!"

Aaron pulled up, hands raised in innocence. "The hell I did! I was *attacked!* I went for help, to *save* everyone. If I hadn't brought in the others, a lot more people might have died."

Celia roared at him, fists balled tight. "We saw you running away, you *coward!* Because of you, a mother and her kid are dead, and Kate is lying here!"

Aaron's hand dropped to his holstered pistol. "Hold on now…" he started, ominously. I realized then that I truly hated Aaron.

The others behind him pressed in closer, but Yolanda already had her gun drawn, and she was seething. "Go ahead, Aaron, make a move." Her pistol vibrated in her white-knuckled hands, tense, energized. It was clear she didn't need any encouragement to kill Aaron, and with Kate subdued, no one was trying to stop her.

Behind Aaron, the others spread out, maybe to avoid the line of fire, or maybe to make it impossible for Yolanda to defend against them all at once.

I had to do something. I jumped in the middle.

"Stop it, all of you!" I said. "We've been through something awful. We've lost people, a child. Let's not make it any worse by fighting each other."

"Yeah, listen to him, everyone," Aaron said, once again feigning compassion. A hack actor on a pretend stage. "Our new doctor here is the one who said we should take the bridge — let's be sure to listen to *him* again!" He pulled out his gun.

And I wheeled on him. Sometimes, combinations of factors work in your favor. This time, the fact that Aaron was at heart a coward, and that I had very little to live for, made it easy for me to swat his gun away in a single gesture. The heavy pistol clattered to the floor, and Aaron looked at me wide-eyed with alarm and dismay. In a low voice, I said, "Get out of here now, Aaron. And don't try me again."

He turned and fled, and his cadre of supporters gradually followed.

7

We stayed the night in the building near the tollbooth, and continued west early the next morning. The day dawned clear but very cold.

Kate recovered surprisingly well. She had scrapes all over, and you could tell she was clenching her jaw to keep from wincing with every step, but she was able to keep moving. Vera and Jacob stayed close to her, often carefully holding her up as she walked. Although the frigid rain had stopped, the air actually felt colder. We kept walking away from the bay, heading west on Route 50. After a while, as the road curved to the left, we saw another bridge, much smaller. Compared to the Bay Bridge, this was nothing but a small arch. A rusting sign nearby said it passed over the Severn River.

Inexplicably, my blood ran cold, freezing my heart for just a moment. I had no reason to dread this place, but I did.

Then, scanning along the bridge, I saw them, toward the middle of the span. First one, then another. Zombies, breathing steam out into the cold air like dragons. They'd come out to forage now that the rain had stopped. They were some distance from us, but we were a big group, with so many people it was nearly impossible to be truly quiet or go unseen. The zombies heard something of interest and with their clouded vision began looking in our direction. They probably couldn't actually see us, but, following their instincts, they began to slowly walk down the bridge, toward us.

"What do you want to do?" I asked Kate. Breathing hard, swaying on her feet, she tried to project an air of strength. It failed. She ended up looking to her advisers with an unexpectedly lost stare. Jacob seemed confused by this new Kate he didn't recognize.

Vera was more pragmatic. She turned to me. "What would you do?" she asked, part plea, part dare.

I put my hand on my shaggy chin. On my wrist was the multicolored bracelet Rosa had made for me, frayed more all the time, but still there. I touched it, as if it would help me decide. Rosa had always seemed so confident in her decisions. I wasn't sure what to do, but I could almost hear her saying, *Help these people. Keep them safe.*

Looking south, I saw three tall, metal towers. Radio towers. Ghosts from a past where communicating with someone on the other side of the world was as common as talking to them face-to-face. Nevertheless, they gave me a direction.

"Kate could use some rest," I said. "Everyone is freezing, and our path is blocked by two zombies —"

"There're three now," Jacob said, jerking his head toward the bridge.

"Okay, three zombies, even worse. We're a big group, but if we cross that bridge now, we'll have to fight them. And the last time we fought zombies, we lost good people." I let that sink in. There were silent nods all around me.

I tilted my head toward the three towers in the distance. "I say we get off this highway for now, go south. Toward those towers. Find some shelter and get some rest, out of the cold."

"Why the towers?" Celia asked, wrinkling her forehead.

"I don't care about the towers per se. It's just a direction to go. There's an exit going south, just behind us, and I can see houses down the river. We can take one of those for a night." I checked to see if anyone disagreed, even Kate, but no one did. "And I want us all in the same building, so we don't have to worry about defending more than one place. Understood?" I realized these last words came out of my mouth like a command.

"Let's do it," Jacob said. I didn't know the kid well, but he was one of Kate's advisers, and a big, strong guy. I was glad to have his support within the group. Vera and Kate both nodded, and we began the process of turning around.

Within a half-hour, we were headed south down the exit ramp. Walking through the woods, I soon felt that I'd made a mistake. Houses weren't plentiful, and the ones we did see were too small, in shambles, no better than sleeping under a tree.

As we emerged from the woods, I could see that we needed a change of direction. In front of us, the highway turned toward the heart of Annapolis via another bridge, but a wide section of its middle was gone, presumably collapsed into the cold waters below. The damage seemed precise, specific, like the bridge was destroyed on purpose. Either way, it meant we turned aside again.

I did it without speaking, knowing that people would object if they realized I was just changing direction at random. So I led the way with an air of purpose, following the road along the side of the river, then turning inland and back among the looming trees. The road narrowed, and grumbling began. Somewhere behind me, I imagined Aaron and his cronies were talking. I knew I had to make good on my plan somehow, and as soon as possible. I continued walking like I knew the way, and thankfully the frequency of houses increased. I was just looking for the right one. But Kate was shuffling, in pain. We needed to rest, and soon.

All of a sudden, the trees cleared and we were standing on the edge of… a *golf course*.

My vision flashed to that little girl, waving to Rosa and me as we drove past the golf course and into The Oasis. The little girl's name was Eva, if I remembered correctly. I wondered where she was now, if she'd made it someplace, to safety.

Then another thought occurred to me. Golf courses have *clubhouses* — usually a good-sized building. A building that could *fit* a hundred people inside. I knew there was a good chance that I was wrong or that the building might be damaged, but I smiled in spite of it all. "Come on!" I said, grinning, a little too enthusiastic. The others looked at me with raised eyebrows, but followed.

The road ran straight through the middle of the golf course, with wide green fairways on either side, now overgrown with long grasses and scattered bushes and trees. With no caretaker, it was returning to the wild, but still it was wide open compared to the forest road we'd left. Up ahead, we spied something unexpected. A double set of chain-link fences stood across our path as far as we could see, from one side to the other. The fences were intact but patched in places with sheets of plywood and other scraps. Along the top of each fence were curls of rusted razor wire. Clearly this was a barrier, something meant to keep things out. Across the path, each fence had a large, rolling gate.

And just beyond, off to the left, there was a long, low brick building with a grey shingle roof. That could only have been the clubhouse.

I led the group toward the fences. As we approached, I kept expecting someone to shout *Halt!* To send us on our way, chased by a hail of gunfire. But nothing happened. There was no movement, and no sound except the accumulated noise of our feet and rolling carts and the cold wind whistling through the surrounding pines.

At the first gate, Jacob reached for the latch. He worked at the mechanism for a moment, then was able to lift it and force the gate to the left by an inch or two, the metal scraping and creaking. "It's open," he said with a shrug. As the gate protested with squeals and shivers, Jacob rolled it farther open and passed through. He repeated the process with the second gate, and we led the group toward the clubhouse. We walked up a driveway that ended in a circle, and I heard something I hadn't heard in a long time.

Faintly, through the faded green double doors of the clubhouse, the sound came. I turned and held up my hands, imploring the group to be quiet. The sentiment was passed around, and at first, the numerous calls of *shhhhh* simply made even more noise, blocking every other sound. But finally, the group fell silent, every eye looking toward the doors.

And we all heard it, distinctly: *music.*

Classical music, wafting lightly through the air. Strains of violins, cellos, clarinets, instruments of a forgotten time, now dead to the world, flittered about, leaving me dumbstruck. How was this possible?

I approached the door, one hand out, slowly, unsure, like I was about to open a doorway in time. My hand trembled as I pulled on the big brass handle, and the heavy door slowly opened outward, hardly making a sound.

The music immediately grew louder. Inside I saw *light.* Electric lights, shaped like the flames of a candle, were blazing in several brass chandeliers hanging from the ceiling of the large, open room. A few tables were scattered about, some surrounded by plush, high-backed chairs in faded light-blue upholstery. And it was *warm.* Blessed heat filled the room and reached out to greet us.

At the same time, the frigid air of the outside gusted into the heated room. From one of the high-backed chairs facing away from us, I saw movement. Leaning over the arm of the tall chair, a little man, late fifties, pudgy, balding with wisps of grey hair, looked at us. Thin metal glasses were perched on his nose, and an open book dangled from his pinkish left hand.

"Oh my," he whispered, then let his mouth hang open as he took in the mass of people suddenly on his doorstep.

8

His name was Oliver. Oliver Rowland. Maybe five-and-a-half-feet tall, chubby in a worn red sweater vest, he stared at us. I felt from the very start that if he could have, he would have cast us out. But there were too many of us. Our need too great, his power too little. Grudgingly, he welcomed us to his home, even offered us some food.

When we'd settled in, every last one of us inside and warming up, I talked to him. Kate sat nearby, but soon faded into sleep. Celia, Jacob, and Vera paid rapt attention, and together we learned his story.

Oliver had been an English professor at the Naval Academy before the outbreak, living along the waterfront beside the road we had just left. When the disease began to spread, the Navy started putting up fences to protect various assets, and this was one of them. Not for the golf course. For the *towers*.

Those three tall spires standing off in the distance were radio towers, known collectively as NSS Annapolis, a naval communications station dating back to the first World War. Oliver told us the station had been rendered useless by satellite technology in the 1990s, but with the world going to hell, the Navy wasn't taking any chances. They set up the fences to protect the station, stocked the place with supplies, and made sure the towers were fully operational.

Oliver said we were on a strip of land protected on three sides by water and on the fourth side by that double line of chain link. The fences ran from one body of water to the other, and he'd patched them up whenever they needed it.

I sat back for a moment, thinking about what that meant for our group. The *options* it gave us. Including one option most likely not available anywhere else. Safety.

Oliver continued his story. As the epidemic got worse, the Navy must have realized that, working or not, some old radio towers weren't a top priority. Something bad happened across the river at the Naval Academy — Oliver didn't know exactly what, faculty had been told to stop reporting not long after the outbreak — and all military personnel were pulled back to better defend the campus. Whoever was out on the peninsula was called back so quickly, they simply left everything behind. As they retreated into the city, they blasted the bridge to avoid having to defend another flank. Eventually, Annapolis, and the Academy itself, fell. Whether it was zombies, infighting, or something else, Oliver didn't know. Soon, he found himself alone in his house by the river.

Oliver, a lifelong bachelor, avid reader, and music aficionado, didn't actually mind. He sort of liked it, even. But he knew the small stash of supplies at his house wouldn't hold, so he approached the double fences, found his way in, and took up residence in the clubhouse.

Much to my dismay, Vera told him about the cure lying dormant in my blood. Oliver's eyes gleamed, but he said nothing. He absorbed it almost as if he'd been expecting the news, with a nod.

He asked us if we'd seen the sports complex building across the way. None of us had. Oliver explained it was several times larger than the clubhouse, and for that reason he didn't try to live there or keep it heated. But the Navy had used it for storage, and it was packed with fuel, food, and water. My mind reeled. Now it was time for our eyes to gleam.

The clubhouse had been Oliver's, and Oliver's alone, for well over six years. In the early days of living there, he told us, he'd had to be diligent. People would come, trying to take what he had. He would run them off, firing blasts from one of several shotguns he kept, always staying safe behind the fences. But he hadn't seen another non-infected human in over a year. He'd tried to maintain discipline, patrolling the fences every hour or two, climbing to the roof of the clubhouse each afternoon to scan the surrounding area, but eventually it became tedious. Finally he just took to reading and listening to music most days. His guard had been let down by complacency.

Hearing him talk, I had a thought. "The radio towers. Do they still work?" I tilted my head, considering what he might answer.

Oliver puffed out his cheeks and took his glasses from his nose. Wiping the lenses on the button-up plaid shirt he wore under his sweater vest, he said, "I don't know. I never tried them. I never had a reason to. And I'm not sure I'd know how to work them even if I wanted to." He put his glasses back on. They gleamed dully. "Why do you ask? Who would you call, anyway?"

I shrugged. I didn't have an answer.

* * *

The place was something magical. I can see why Oliver stayed, even alone. It was *comfortable*, in a way that none of us had expected. The first day turned into two. Then four. Then a week and more. With the fence keeping us safe, we were free to explore the peninsula. We took supplies from the sports complex, and used them to set up living quarters.

Because of the clubhouse's layout, we ended up with two areas where people slept, one at the north end, another at the south. Oliver's own small room was in the north section, and maybe because of that, Kate chose a place nearby. Whether that was out of respect or a desire to keep an eye on him, I didn't know. But Celia, Jacob, Vera, and I did the same, making little homey areas in the north wing. Human nature being what it is, Aaron and his counterparts took up residence on the south side.

The vast majority of our group maintained no special allegiance and simply filled in wherever there was space. What did they care about Kate or Aaron, or me for that matter, when for the first time since Norfolk they were safe and warm and well-fed. But one thing was clear. The people in power were on one side of the clubhouse. The people who wanted power were on the other side.

* * *

The sports complex building was huge, many times the size of the clubhouse. Its roof and walls were intact, and although it wasn't heated, it was a hell of a lot more comfortable than being outside in the cold. I remembered the school Rosa and I had found as we trekked along the interstate, a tiny reflection of an oasis. I imagined the sports complex could be that one day. I began to feel obligated to give the gift I carried in my veins to more people. We had so much — I had so much — and now there was the chance to share a cure. Rosa's memory tugged at my mind, urging me to spread the word. But how?

The answer literally towered over me each day as I walked the roads of the peninsula. The radio towers.

I gathered Kate, Celia, Oliver, and the others. "What would it take to get those towers running?" I asked.

Oliver rolled his eyes. "This again?" he asked. "How would —"

Kate cut him off. "Why?"

"I want to send a message to DC," I said. "Tell them to come here. Let us help them."

"*What?*" Oliver looked panicked. "Bring all those people here? Are you crazy? We don't have space or resources for an entire city to come *here*."

"Why not?" I asked. "We have the sports complex. It's, what, fifty or sixty thousand square feet. I mean, depending on how many people come here, they might be stacked up like cord wood, but there's space. There's two other houses farther down the peninsula. And we could build."

Oliver scoffed, but Kate, a bead of sweat on her upper lip, considered it. "We could also push out the walls," she said. "There are houses nearby, outside the fence. But we'd have to be self-sufficient. How do we do that?"

A silence came over the group. Then Celia chimed in, eyeing me. "Well, we were growing crops on the Eastern Shore. We'd have to find seed, which could be pretty hard. But those big lawns out there, the fairways, might make good fields for planting." I grinned, proud of her, thinking it was a pretty good idea. The city kid who'd blistered her hands working her first field a few months back was now teaching these other folks a thing or two about surviving in the outside world.

"This is *preposterous!*" Oliver said, chubby cheeks reddening. "You can't possibly think that bringing thousands of people here is a good idea. We'd starve in weeks!"

"There's more," I said, stopping Oliver's complaint. "We *need* them to come. The only way we can take the cure in my veins and give it to everyone else is by finding someone who knows how to *do* that. I don't. And unless you're keeping something from me, neither do any of you. We need people from DC. Specifically, from NIH — the researchers who have been working on a cure for the last 10 years. Now we have one we can drop in their laps. We just need them to figure out how to share it." Even Oliver, who clearly missed his days of solitude, didn't have anything to say to that. The idea of being cured was something none of us could discount.

Celia spoke again. "About the towers. We may have people here already who can help with them. People who worked for the Navy in Norfolk. Engineers."

A dawn of understanding broke over Kate. "That's true. Reginald is one. And… the tall guy, with the dark hair that's starting grey — what's his name?"

"Dennis?" Vera offered.

"That's him," Kate said. "He's always tinkering with something. He might know how to get those towers back up and running." She looked around, grinning.

"So," I said, "we're agreed to try?"

"No!" Oliver crossed his arms, a spoiled child who wasn't getting his way. "No, we are *not* agreed!"

"Well, we'll vote then. All in favor?"

Every hand was raised. Except Oliver's.

9

Reginald and Dennis, the engineers, were joined by two former Navy communications specialists, Blake and Emily. Together, they worked nonstop to get the towers back online. The idea that their work might directly help cure the infection had them fired up. We didn't need to do anything more to coax them.

There was a building at the base of the northernmost tower, and inside was a generator, an insurance policy left by the Navy. The four of them were able to clean it up, fuel it, and get it running. It gave them a communications headquarters and also powered the tower above it. They started calling their building Comm Center. With it up and running, they were ready to try broadcasting.

For our first test, Kate, Oliver, Celia and I joined Dennis, Reginald, Blake, and Emily at Comm Center. I'd found an old battery-powered radio and the batteries to run it. Turning it on, I scanned the airwaves. All across the radio dial, I found nothing but static. Then Dennis tried the first transmission.

We had to use Morse code. It was the only option, given the situation. In a way, my heart sank. We were asking a lot. Whoever was out there had to be able to pick up our transmission, know what they were hearing, find a way to translate it, then have the guts to pack up and come to us. But it was better than nothing.

As Dennis tapped out the message, I held my hand on the tuner of the radio, expecting to have to search the dial for the transmission. But I didn't need to bother. The second Dennis made his first tap, the sound came out of my radio like a gunshot. I jumped up and yelled in surprise. Joy overcame us, and we began hugging each other. But Oliver stood off to one side alone, and Reginald and Dennis were reserved. "Don't get too excited," Reginald said. "It's loud because we're right underneath the tower. Who knows if they'll hear it in DC?"

Our enthusiasm faded, and we got down to business. Blake and Emily took over the desk. They set up a schedule. They would trade shifts, tapping out our message, hoping someone would hear it.

Near Annapolis. Three towers by river. Need medical researchers to spread cure from blood. Come to us.

* * *

Outside, the dark early winter was upon us as we made the frigid walk through the woods back to the clubhouse. The air smelled of coming snowfall, and the moon made a fuzzy white glow behind ominous clouds.

Dennis and Reginald, finally allowing themselves to bubble at their success, walked briskly in front. Celia and I trailed them, with Kate walking stiffly behind. Oliver sulked at the back.

Through the woods we walked, Dennis dismissing the silence of the trees with his exuberant, excited talk. Reginald laughed and followed suit.

Suddenly I heard Kate gasp. Celia and I wheeled about, only to see Oliver rushing toward Kate with a pistol drawn.

Time froze.

Kate flinched, backed away. Celia and I only had time to turn and watch. Why hadn't I anticipated this? We had taken away Oliver's privacy, his home. We were threatening to bring untold masses of people down upon him. Everything he'd held dear for six years was turned upside-down. He thrust the pistol out — a gun we didn't even know he carried, given the protected nature of our location — with Kate's life in his hands.

And he fired.

Still stiff from her injuries, Kate flailed wildly, fell to the ground. A hideous shriek. The sounds of pain and death. The burnt smell of gunpowder. Oliver ran up, gun pointed down at the ground.

Not at Kate. *Beside* her.

There, next to Kate, a milky-eyed raccoon convulsed in the grass, dying. Kate rolled away from it, bumping over the root she had tripped on, dumbfounded, incredulous at what had happened. Reginald and Dennis could only stare.

Oliver stood over the raccoon with no mercy. Another explosion tore through the silent, dark night, and reflexively we all covered our ears. Then the raccoon was still. A tiny twist of smoke floated up and away from Oliver's pistol, into the cold moonlight. He looked at us slowly. "I think it was rabid," he said, panting. "It was coming for Kate."

I looked at the raccoon. There was no way to be sure, but the thick look of its skin, especially around the face, made me believe it was true. "Not just rabies, I think. RL2013."

Oliver's eyes grew wide with alarm. "That… is that *possible?*" he asked.

I just nodded, reaching out a hand to help Kate up.

10

"Oliver," Kate said in a quiet voice, almost timid. "Thank you. You might've saved my life." She reached out a hand.

Oliver waved it off. "I just saw it was... you know... it was going to *bite* you, and I, well, I thought I shouldn't let it *do* that." He fumbled his hands awkwardly as he spoke, then turned away shyly.

"Well, thank you, again," Kate said.

"Are you all right?" I asked her.

She nodded, seeming unsure. "Yeah, yeah. Just startled me. But..."

"But what?" I asked, frowning. It wasn't like Kate to be unsure or confused. I didn't like where this seemed to be headed.

"Well, my mouth. It feels strange. Tight." She rubbed at her jaw with her hand.

"Let's get back," I said. "It's cold out." We continued toward the clubhouse, this time in a tighter group.

As we walked, I thought of what Kate said. My natural instinct as a doctor was to figure out what it meant, why it was happening. It didn't take me long to reach a likely conclusion: tetanus. The rebar that had jabbed into Kate's side, sheared and rusty, could easily have exposed her to tetanus. And that was bad. Very, very bad.

Tetanus is fatal if untreated, and I had no way to treat the infection. If I had the right *medicines*, maybe, but I didn't. I would need to keep a close watch on her. If it got worse, I'd have to consider going into Annapolis, looking for drugs.

We stepped into the clubhouse. Within moments, an eruption of happiness swept over the group, sparked by the tale of the first radio transmission, and even by Oliver's unexpected rescue of Kate. Only one thing dampened the group's spirit. If there was an infected raccoon inside our gates, what else could appear? We'd have to be more careful.

Still, people laughed and enjoyed themselves, sounds of happiness that this part of the world probably hadn't heard in a long time. The revelry continued into the night.

Kate sat off to one side. Listening and sometimes smiling, but never really joining in.

* * *

The next day, Kate could barely open her mouth. She sat at one of the tables, seemingly asleep. I knew what I had to do.

I took Celia, Jacob, and Vera aside. "We have to go into Annapolis," I said. "I need to see if I can find some medicine to help Kate."

"What's wrong with her?" Vera asked.

"I can hear you, you know," Kate said, opening her eyes but not raising her head from the table.

I turned to face her. "Kate. I think you have tetanus." I could tell from her expression that she regarded this as a trivial concern. "It's serious." She looked surprised. I kept at it. "Back before the outbreak, tetanus was *nothing*. A little medicine, and *boom*, everything was okay. But *now*. We don't have the medicine. Tetanus can kill you." Everyone suddenly got my point. The air ran out of the room.

Celia spoke first. "Okay, let's go then. Get some medicine." I looked toward her and gave her a smile. She was fearless, like always.

"We have to try," I said. "I have no idea if we'll find anything, but we'll go."

"Then it's me and you," Celia said, considering it a done deal.

"No, Celia. I want you here for Kate, for the group," I said. She started to object, but I held up my hand and turned. "Jacob and Vera. Will you take me into Annapolis? Watch my back? Help me help Kate?" As Kate's closest, most trusted advisers, I knew they couldn't refuse. They both simply nodded.

Celia looked at me angrily, but I wouldn't meet her eyes. There was no point arguing. I wanted someone I could trust holding down the fort.

* * *

Before we set out for Annapolis, Oliver gave us some advice. He suggested we try buildings just north of the highway, right after we crossed the bridge. There were a number of medical buildings there, he said. We'd have more options.

The trip itself was uneventful. We went back to the main highway and turned west, crossing the bridge. The zombies, the ones who had thwarted us before, seemed to have left the area, at least temporarily.

We spent a whole day searching through anything that looked remotely like it might hide a stash of medicine. We saw a good number of zombies here and there as we traveled around, but we were few and silent. We avoided them.

We searched from building to building, collecting small medical supplies and a number of different drugs, intent on bringing anything we could find back to the group. Finally, we found a small supply of Valium. It was a depressant but also a muscle relaxant. It would help with Kate's symptoms. But it wasn't a cure. My worry increased.

By early evening, I suspected we'd found everything we were going to find. We headed back over the bridge and home.

* * *

I walked into the clubhouse's main room to find it spilling over with life. Families played card games together. Other people sat and talked. The sense of normalcy was as apparent as it was odd. To the side, Kate sat asleep, pretty much where she'd been when we left. I went to her and touched her shoulder, and she opened her eyes.

"Hi," she said, still fogged with sleep. "What's the good news?" She forced a smile.

"Here, take one of these," I said, holding out a pill. Vera offered water to help rinse it down.

"What is it?" Kate asked.

"Valium."

"How long do I have to take it, you know… to get better?" She still wore a slight smile, but her eyes betrayed her deeper concern.

I squeezed her shoulder, summoning my old bedside manner. "We'll see. Take this now, and we'll see how it helps you." I smiled, hoping she couldn't see through me.

Suddenly Dennis skidded up in front of us. "Celia," he said, panting.

"What is it?" I asked.

"I don't want to alarm you if it's nothing, but... she's gone."

* * *

"Split up, look everywhere," I said, marching through the building. "Where was she last?" I asked Dennis over my shoulder.

He jogged to keep up with me. "Emily was on shift at Comm Center, and Celia said she wanted to check on her. After a couple of hours, we were surprised she didn't come back, so I went over there. Emily says she never saw her."

"Is anyone else missing?" I said. "I mean, is there anyone else conspicuously out of sight today?"

Dennis thought. "Yeah, now that you mention it. I haven't seen that nurse, Renee. Or..." He set his jaw. "Aaron."

I started to run.

* * *

The clubhouse was big enough for our group, but it wasn't endless. It wasn't long before we'd checked it thoroughly and found nothing. The sports complex was a lot bigger, but most of that was one big, open room. Within an hour, we had that cleared, too.

What else was there?

"You said you went to Comm Center?" I asked Dennis.

"Yeah, she's definitely not there," he said.

That left someplace outside the fence.

Or those two empty houses by the other towers.

* * *

Dennis and I hurried to the houses, joined by Jacob and Vera, each of whom carried a pistol. The other three were younger than me by decades and had to slow down, waiting for me. As we made our way down the path, the dark woods closed in on both sides. If we didn't find them in one of the houses... if we had to check the *woods*.... Eventually, the four of us stood in front of the two seemingly abandoned buildings, as scattered flakes of snow started to drift down around us.

"We're going inside," I said, puffing bursts of white breath into the frosty air. "Two in each building. One through the front and one through the back. Dennis, Jacob, take that one." I pointed to the house on the left, a nondescript brick structure with patches of aluminum siding. "Vera and I will take the other one."

Dennis and Jacob immediately went their way, and we went ours. I silently motioned to Vera that I would take the front. She nodded, crept around to the back. I stepped up to the front door.

It was unlocked and opened easily. That bothered me more than if it had been locked up tight. Directly inside the door, there was a short hallway. I began to walk down the hallway, toward a point about halfway along, where doors opened on the left and right. A sound that I couldn't quite place came from somewhere down the hall, and I stepped quietly to find its source. A sound like plastic, slightly crinkling?

It wasn't dark inside the house, but dim. Dim enough to obscure my sight. As I reached the juncture with the doors, I peered first into the one on the left. Just an old, empty room. An overturned chair, stuffing pulled out of it. A small end table coated with a thick layer of dust. I turned to the right and again saw nothing. Another old room littered with artifacts from time gone by. A broken lamp, shade crumpled and off kilter, lying on the floor.

Then I heard another sound.

A shuffling sound. Feet. Sliding across the gritty floor, scraping like fine sandpaper. It came from in front of me, from behind a door at the end of the hall. The door stood ajar by an inch or two. I moved up, placed my hand on the scarred wood surface, gently pushed it open.

Inside, I saw two bodies splayed out, one on a table, the other beside it on a couch. Another person stood at the far side of the room, back turned toward me.

The one on the table, lying still, as if in a dream, was Celia.

Lower, on the couch, Aaron mirrored her position, eyes closed.

And turned away from me, the nurse, Renee, worked at something on a counter up against the back wall. Idly, she shifted her weight, and her foot slid a few inches across the floor, making that gritty sound. *Shhhhk.*

I saw tubes connecting Celia and Aaron, and a dark flow of blood was passing from her to him.

The bastard, the *coward*, Aaron, was taking Celia's blood.

"What the hell do you think you're doing?" I thundered. Renee wheeled around, Aaron's eyes flew open.

Renee moved toward me, and I immediately tensed for an attack, fists raised. But she darted past me, eyes huge and bulging in fear. She ran into the hallway and was gone, out of the house.

Celia was unconscious, but I could see she was breathing. She appeared to be drugged.

Aaron looked at me, unsure of what to do.

"This ends *now*," I said, and, reaching down, pulled the needle out of Celia's arm. That's when Aaron launched himself at me.

We fell, him on top, and slammed to the floor, sliding through the dust and dirt, piling up against the wall. He reached for my throat and I pushed and punched at him, trying anything to keep him from gaining hold. Above us, I saw Celia's arm dripping red. I knew I had to stop the flow, apply pressure, so she wouldn't lose more blood. Who knew how long the transfusion had already been going on? Every drop was her life, falling away.

Aaron and I rolled, and out of simple desperation, I managed to slip free and stagger to my feet. Aaron scrambled up, slapped at a counter nearby, finding an old letter opener. He raised the rusty metal blade and pointed it toward me. I had nothing. He approached, a smile on his face.

There was a sound like thunder in the small room, and Aaron died with that smile still on his face, his body knocked to the far wall. Vera stood in the doorway, the smoking gun held steadily in her hand. She looked around quickly for any other threats, then stepped into the room.

I rushed to Celia's side, applying pressure to the site where the needle had been ripped out. Then I scanned the room, zeroing in on the counter, where Renee had been organizing medical supplies when I walked in. I saw a bandage. "Get me that!" I pointed, and Vera grabbed the package. After a few minutes, Celia was safe, bandaged, but still unconscious from whatever drugs they'd given her.

Dennis and Jacob soon joined us, and together we carried Celia back to the clubhouse. We left Aaron behind, food for whatever vermin found him later, assuming they could stand the taste.

* * *

We walked slowly, partially from exhaustion and partially to keep Celia as comfortable as possible. Jacob did most of the carrying, but the rest of us helped.

As we approached the clubhouse, we heard a commotion by the gates of the outer fence. The weather was bitter cold, so I was surprised to see so many of our group outside. Some of them were even in t-shirts and shorts, like they had no idea they were going to be outside.

I asked Jacob to take Celia inside and find her a comfortable place, and to keep his eyes open for Renee. He nodded, headed for the clubhouse. Then I walked into the crowd by the gates.

Pushing my way through, I got closer to the inner fence. And I saw something glinting in the muted twilight.

A car.

There, outside our fence, sat a dull blue car, pockmarked with brown rust, but with chrome parts seeming to glow in the shadows. Its engine was off, but from the sweet smell of its exhaust, familiar and unexpected, I could tell it had been running recently. Both doors stood open, and beside the car on my right stood a young man, early twenties, with a shock of dark hair and thick glasses. On the other side of the car was a pretty, young woman, reddish hair, wearing a thick green coat. But under that coat… her *clothes*. And his. They looked like those quasi uniforms we had in the city.

I was stunned. The hesitant flurries of snow left flecks of white in their hair, on their shoulders.

"What's going on here?" I asked.

Someone near me, a young boy in faded jean shorts and a ripped grey t-shirt with the letters USNA written in deep blue, said, "They just drove up! They're from DC!"

I moved to the front, to the inner gates. I started to open my mouth, but, exhausted, realized I couldn't figure out what to say.

Then the young man by the car spoke. "Is this The Oasis?" he asked with a hesitant smile, eyes so full of hope and joy that I thought he might burst from the effort to keep them contained.

And I thought of The Oasis, the *real* Oasis. Of those people in South Carolina, offering a cure. Of Harvey, and Marian. Of Hank and Janine. And of Rosa.

A cure. Offering a cure. Wasn't that what we were doing? Wasn't that what our radio message promised? I looked at my feet for a second, then looked back up at the young man, maybe a third of my age. Who was I to shatter his dreams? And weren't we exactly what he was looking for, anyway?

"Yeah, I guess it is, now," I said.

"Welcome to Oasis, Maryland."

11

Life at the new Oasis fell into the repetition of habit. The winter dragged on, but we didn't mind. Our supplies held. In fact, they seemed almost endless. But Kate and I didn't trust them to last forever. We asked for volunteers to serve as scouts, and they went into Annapolis regularly, and to some places even farther out, to gather anything they could find. Food, water, medicine, and fuel were our top priorities. And the scouts found stores of seed that we held on to, readying for spring, hoping to plant in the fields that surrounded us.

Celia recovered within a day. Luckily, the transfusion hadn't been underway for long when I found her. She told us about her ordeal. Aaron snuck up on her as she walked the path to Comm Center alone, drugging her with something provided by Renee. The look in her eye when she described him grabbing her from behind told me it was a terrifying reminder of her previous encounter with

Aaron and Burt — the reason she set off alone in the first place. I'd heard enough and didn't want her to have to relive any more of her nightmare. "It doesn't matter," I said. "You're here now, and Aaron is dead."

Renee was another story. It was the first time any of us had to decide such a thing. What did we do with someone who couldn't be trusted to remain with the group? Kill her? Improvise some sort of jail? Or even send her out, banish her? We considered everything, and in the end did nothing. We still needed a nurse, and in the world of the infection, survival trumped justice. We knew we had to keep our eyes on her, but that was it.

Then there was Kate. Tetanus had a hold of her, and she was suffering. The Valium helped ease the symptoms, but it wasn't making her any better. She spent her time either rigid and in pain, or doped and asleep. Eating and drinking became torturous. Vera was a saint, sticking by Kate, helping her in any way she could. Keeping her fed, giving her water. Keeping her alive.

Several more cars arrived from DC, those black, nondescript government sedans, but filled with refugees, not federal agents. A big white van came in, loaded with two families. The people told us that DC was in turmoil. The government had fallen, or at least retreated to somewhere none of them knew anything about. What remained were pockets of people banded together inside the city walls, trying to live. The power was out. Only folks with battery-powered radios had a chance to hear us, if they even bothered to listen.

Oliver heard all this and argued it was time to stop wasting fuel running the towers. I ignored him. And, without anyone asking, Blake and Emily changed the message.

Near Annapolis. Three towers by river. Need medical researchers to spread cure from blood. Come to The Oasis.

I asked every one of the newcomers about NIH — if they knew of any researchers left in DC, or if there was anyone still working for a cure. No one had any idea.

Days went by, and weeks. Our numbers grew slowly, with refugees continuing to trickle in, mostly from DC. By midwinter, we had doubled the size of our group. The hardier arrivals, more adventurous, set up their living quarters in the sports complex. It remained unheated, but they were able to make it work. They called it indoor camping. During the day, the main room of the clubhouse was typically overrun with people. Talking, idly playing games, just staying warm.

The scouts brought in a small but steady stream of additional supplies, but their excursions weren't without risk.

One afternoon, there was shouting at the gates. A pair of scouts had returned, and were rushed inside. People called for me, for a nurse. At the fence I found one of the scouts, a man so young he looked to me like a child, holding the side of his face, blood all over him, red and black in blotches.

Instinct took over. "Carry him inside and tell me what happened." It had been a zombie, of course. They didn't see it coming until it had a hold on the kid and was biting into his ear. The second scout, slightly older and bulkier, killed it. But the kid was bitten. Everyone knew what that meant. My nostrils filled with the metallic smell of blood mixed with the musty sweat and sour breath of the kid as I leaned in close.

"You..." the kid started, hesitantly looking up at me as I cleaned the wound. "You can... *save* me, right?" He offered a weak, hopeful smile that turned into a wincing grimace as I used alcohol to disinfect his ragged ear.

I stood up straight. It had been weeks — a couple of months? — since I'd saved Celia, but was that enough time? I had given her an awful lot of blood, more than a standard transfusion. But the kid was going to turn. All I could do was try.

* * *

We set up a clean space. Other than myself, Renee seemed to be our resident expert on how to get it done, so I made her help, under careful supervision from Celia, Jacob, and Vera. We didn't say it out loud, but I think we all considered this to be Renee's chance for at least partial redemption.

I was one table in the clubhouse, the young scout next to me on another. Renee swabbed our arms with alcohol wipes, sank needles into them, her touch surprisingly gentle, and that's all I really remember before I passed out. I wasn't ready, my *body* wasn't ready yet. Jacob told me later that Renee tried to keep going, but Celia made her stop.

A couple of days later, the kid turned and Jacob took him into the woods. Around the clubhouse, almost 200 people sat silent and staring as the distant gunshot ripped through the air and echoed across the river.

12

A day went by. No one said much of anything, each of us just going about our own routine. A somber mood filled the clubhouse, a poisonous gas that choked out everything else. In corners of the room, you could hear sobs. I felt like a failure. I had let the kid down. Let him die. I never even learned his name.

The following afternoon, I was sitting by a window in the clubhouse, fingering the ragged knots on my bracelet, when I heard a gasp from the other side of the room. Looking over, I could see people standing around a figure lying on the floor. Peering between their shuffling legs, I saw Kate, her back arched horribly. Tired and weak, I ambled over, but there was nothing to be done. I went to her anyway, crouched down, felt for a pulse on her neck. It was thready, almost gone. *This is it*, I thought. With one last, awful seizing clench of her muscles, her body twisted and stretched, then gave way. Her last breath tumbled out of her like a balloon deflating, and she didn't move again,

The group, already in shock, collapsed in dismay. Old fears, tamped down during the long march from Norfolk, now sprang free. Some people broke down, some lashed out. Arguments started. There was even a fistfight somewhere toward the south wing.

I began to speak, but my throat was dry, rough. Gravelly and low, I said, "That's *enough*." A couple of people near me turned, but the group was too big. Most didn't hear me. So I tried again, louder, stronger. "That's enough!" More heads turned toward me, and over the course of several awkward moments, everyone stopped and fell silent, looking to me.

"Enough tears. Enough fighting. Stop it! If you want something to fight, let's fight for our lives!" I didn't know what I was going to say. The words were coming out on their own. I had everyone's attention. So I made a decision, right then and there. I took a blanket from a sofa nearby and gently spread it over Kate, taking care to cover her face. I bowed my head for a short, solitary moment, then stood up and turned back toward the group. "We need to act," I said. "We need to stop sitting back here, in relative comfort, *hoping* something is going to happen. That someone is going to show up and save us. It's not going to happen. We need to save ourselves. Kate died because we don't have the right medicines. That kid died because we don't know how to spread the cure, even though it's sitting right here. In my own veins. I want to cure all of you, but I don't know how."

I paused to let that sink in. People blinked, or folded their arms, or held on to one another, but I had no idea if I was getting through to anyone. "It's time for us to go to DC and find what we need," I said. "The right people and the right machines to take my blood and turn it into something that can cure everyone. We can't stop every disease, every infection, every accident or tragedy, but we can stop this one." I took a breath, thinking. *God, am I ready for this?* But what else was there to do? "I'm going into DC. I used to live there, and I know my way around, at least parts of it. I'm going to find what we need to spread the cure and bring it back here."

A murmur ran through the crowd. Finally, a reaction. Then someone spoke up, a man's voice, from the back where I couldn't see his face. "You can't go. You're *in charge now.*"

Now it was my turn to blink. What the hell was this? In charge? Then others joined in, calling out, "We need you!" "With Kate gone, you've *got* to be our leader."

My eyes scanned the room, seeing imploring faces looking back at me. Then I saw Oliver, off to one side, simply staring at me, his eyes squinting slighting through his round glasses. I shouted to stop the noise. "You don't need me to lead you *here*," I said, "doing nothing, doing the same thing every day until we die. I need to go to DC. I need to get this done. If no one will come with me, I'll go alone."

"I'll go with you." Celia stepped out of the group to stand next to me, and I offered her a small smile of thanks, nodding my head like a little bow. The two of us would be back on the road again, like old times.

Then another voice spoke up. "I'll go, too."

It was Oliver.

* * *

The various newcomers from DC gave us all the news they could. They knew where to find some people, the ones who wouldn't join them when they left, but they didn't know any researchers. They warned us about the dangers. There were now infected roaming the city, inside the walls. It wasn't safe to wander.

I thought about how things had changed. Rosa and I, we had left a city that, while stifling and strict, at least *functioned*. Then we went back and stood outside the walls and Rosa made an announcement that apparently broke the spell, woke everyone up, and ended 10 years of totalitarian rule. How many people had died in the ensuing months?

The irony that Rosa delivered a message of hope and salvation, only to have untold numbers of people perish rather than be saved, was heart-wrenching. I knew she wouldn't have wanted it that way. But it wasn't her fault. All she did was try to help.

I wondered if I was about to make a similar mistake, to somehow damn these people to a fate I couldn't predict.

I didn't know what the future held, whether I would have any luck. Like Rosa, all I could do was try.

13

We decided on the big white van. It had enough gas to get us to DC and back, and room enough to carry me, Celia, and Oliver, a few other people, and some gear, assuming we found anything worth bringing back. Two men joined us — a thin, olive-skinned guy with a haze of black stubble across his chin named Ray, and a taller, round-faced one named Zachary. They brought long rifles that they kept slung over their shoulders like they were going on safari. I drove, with Celia next to me in the front passenger seat. Oliver, Ray, and Zachary sat on the floor in the open back of the van, leaning against the walls. We all carried a small supply pack with water, some food, a few spare items of clothing, and whatever else each of us felt was important. Plus, Celia and I each carried a loaded pistol. We offered Oliver a gun, but he waved it off.

The entire group, 200 or so strong, came out to see us off in the morning, waving as we drove out through the double gates. I could see a mix of emotions, as some people smiled and cheered, while others couldn't hold back their tears. I felt both emotions myself: excitement over the chance to try to change things, but a looming fear of the unknown dangers ahead.

We drove north, through the woods, then up the ramp and onto the main highway, where we turned west toward DC.

As we drove, the noises of the road drowned out the sounds of Ray and Zachary talking in the back. Oliver seemed to be sitting quietly, or might have been asleep.

After a while, Celia cleared her throat. I noticed she had kept her head shaven, more neatly than before, without the cuts and scrapes. She must have decided to keep this new style, this reborn person she had become. Reborn like magic, from my blood. I couldn't help but think of her like a daughter, with a mixture of pride and love. As well as a deep concern for her safety. Maybe I shouldn't have let her come along.

"Do you ever wonder if there's any point at all?" she asked, looking off through the windshield at the passing landscape.

I uttered a single, surprised laugh. "*Ever?* Do I ever wonder that? Heck, that's all I think about." I gave another small chuckle.

Celia turned to look at me. "Really? You're kidding." She actually seemed surprised. "But you're the one who's always moving forward, getting things done. You don't get bogged down by what's happened, you move on to what's next." She said it like she was trying to convince me.

I shrugged, keeping both hands on the wheel as I slowed to navigate around several abandoned cars. My bracelet, Rosa's weave of many colors, still clung like a promise around my wrist, but frayed and stretched. "I can't explain that," I said. "Sometimes my body keeps moving, and I'm just a passenger along for the ride."

"Well, you had me fooled." Celia sighed. After a moment, she added, "What do you think of this business of you being in charge?"

I drove in silence for a minute or two, watching the passing pines along the side of the road. "You know," I said, "I think *that's* what fuels my body to keep moving, even if I don't consciously think about it." I rubbed my forehead, thinking back. "Before I met Rosa, I just looped the same day, endlessly. Ten years of repetition, doing what I was told, when I was told to do it. Then *she* was there, and things changed. I moved forward. And before you arrived, before Addy arrived, at that house, I was pretty much done. I'd stopped caring and stopped moving. But with you and the dog, I regained some purpose. Internally, something took over, and I got back to work. Now, with all these people back at our new Oasis, I don't know if I'm smart enough to be their leader or not, but it gives me something to do. Keeps me moving."

"Don't you ever want to stop?" she said. "Just to relax?"

"No. Not really." I moved my hands higher up on the wheel, stared down at the bracelet. "Not anymore."

14

We fell into silence as we drove along, weaving among the remains of a dead civilization. Celia seemed lost in her thoughts; I retreated to my own.

In the back, Ray and Zachary finally went quiet, staring out at the never-ending landscape of buildings, stores, cars. I had the feeling that for them, it was less about the regret of seeing objects from days gone by and more about the sheer anomaly of it all.

And Oliver slept.

Driving only my second vehicle in the past 10 years, I couldn't help but be reminded of the RV, and of Rosa. Those thoughts increased my mental isolation from the group, my self-imposed quiet. I realized I had a new regret, and it was almost bottomless. While I had told Rosa my feelings for her, I'd never been proactive. All that time at The Oasis, I let her spend her days on research. The work she did was important for us all — hell, for everyone in the world — but ultimately it was short-lived. I never stopped her and asked for at least a little time for us just to be together. I thought farther back, to those days in her mother's apartment in DC. The times we shared then were possibly the happiest of my life. And I remembered how I'd started to avoid those moments, avoid her, fearing her growing fascination with The Oasis.

I pounded the steering wheel of the van with one fist, lightly, a hollow echo of my mental mood. Celia snapped out of her daze. "What?" she asked. "What is it?" Her eyes studied me.

I gave her a quick look, then tried to shrug off my distress. "Uh, nothing. Nothing," I said. "I just... hope this works." My half-hearted grin and inability to meet her eyes told the real story. But she knew me. She stayed quiet.

* * *

A short while later, I eased the van to a stop. The congestion of abandoned and destroyed cars had increased steadily as we reached DC, but, approaching what must have been the city's easternmost wall, I saw that they jammed every available space. We weren't within sight of DC, but still we had to abandon the van and walk.

I felt like we hiked for miles, past hundreds and hundreds of cars, and who knew how many twisted, desiccated corpses. Dozens of cats, dogs, and rats skittered off as we passed by. I was surprised none of them seemed infected, and wondered how long that would last.

Then we saw it. The wall.

Built into an old overpass, the wall was sheer metal from the ground up, towering several stories over our heads. The government had been thorough. The walls of the original Oasis, or even the formidable structure I remembered glimpsing outside Richmond, before they started shooting at us, were like a child's fort next to this massive bulwark. I looked left and right, and saw the wall's smoothly armored flank curve away from us in both directions, fading into the distance through the leafless trees.

For a moment, I held my breath, expecting the worst. Images arose in my mind of Rosa frantically wheeling the RV around after someone on the walls of Richmond fired on us. And of Rosa falling to the ground maybe a few miles from here, gunned down in Virginia, just outside DC's western border. But there was no one here, not a soul.

I thought back to when I first entered the newly fortified city, at the beginning of the epidemic. A sudden memory came to me. *This is just for a little while*, I had told myself, standing in the long line of people streaming into DC. *Until things calm down.* How wrong I was. After 10 years, millions upon millions dead, an entire civilization in shambles, things had not calmed down yet. And they didn't look to be calming down any time soon.

When I came to DC, I'd arrived from this same direction, on this very same road. But it was before the wall was anything like the metal beast it had become. Back then, it was a chain-link fence, with a couple of gates. It looked more like the camp we'd just left outside Annapolis, but swarming with military. Now the wall was huge and solid, but devoid of life.

Puffing out white clouds in the cold air, we made our way forward. Ray and Zachary guarded our flanks, guns drawn. Celia stayed close to me, while Oliver seemed to drift in his own cocoon.

Unable to go through or over the wall, all we could do was pick a direction and follow it, hoping for a break. In places, the government had been frugal, using existing buildings to complete parts of the structure rather than creating everything from scratch. Luckily for us, those old, decaying, red-brick buildings were a weak point. It wasn't long before we found one where the doors and windows had been knocked out, and we passed through the wall's perimeter with ease.

We stepped into a dark maze of abandoned rooms heavy with the damp smell of concrete, dust and age thick in the air. Celia drew her pistol, but I kept mine tucked away in my waistband. My eyes slowly adjusted to the dim light as we slipped from one room into a hallway, down through another room, and onward. Trying to find a way through to the other side, into DC.

As we entered a third room, Oliver tripped on a pile of debris — crumbled brick from the walls, bits of plaster from the ceiling — and fell. In the empty building, it sounded like thunder. He immediately jumped up and wiped himself off, fumbling and apologetic.

As we regrouped, I thought I heard something from back in the hallway. I held up a hand. "*Shhh*, wait a second. *Quiet.*" Ray and Zachary held their guns ready, looking in every direction for a target, but finding nothing. We all froze, but heard nothing else.

On the far side of the room was a small office set off by a wooden door. Beside the door was a large window, streaked and dirty now, but I imagined some supervisor, in the time before the infection, sitting on the other side of the glass, watching workers in the main room go about whatever their tasks had been. The window was caked with grime, but a distinct light was filtering through. I opened the door and the light grew stronger. Through another filthy window, we could see the warm glow of sunlight. There was a door on the far side of the room that looked to open to the outside.

Anxious to get out of the building and into the city, I went quickly to the door.

The old metal knob turned with a gritty sound, most of the way around, but not enough to clear the latch and open. I tried a second time as the others piled into the small office behind me.

Celia stood by the window, trying to peer through the filmy surface.

On my second try, the knob turned farther, *scritch scritch scritch*, and some of the grit seemed to loosen. I shouldered into the door with a *thud*, hoping to jar it loose. I turned and pulled at the knob with all my strength, willing it to open.

Beside me, Celia's face was just an inch from the dirty glass pane as she squinted and said, "Hold on. There's something mov—"

The glass shattered inward as a large infected man with milky white eyes and a bloody gash across his left cheek burst through, tumbling into the room and nearly toppling onto Celia. She screamed, her pistol clattering away across the dusty floor as she fell back.

The knob clicked in my hand and the door swung open, revealing a small courtyard. Outside, I saw four more zombies scrabbling toward us in their feral way. Before I could close the door, their hands were clawing at the frame. I stepped away.

"Get back!" I shouted as Ray pulled up his gun, trying to get a clear shot. In the small room, with so many of us jostling for space, humans and zombies, any gunshot likely would do more harm than good. Zachary seemed to realize this, and flipped his rifle around to wield it like a club. But the size of the room prevented that, too. Pushing back out of the office and into the main room, we staggered away from our attackers.

And into an ambush.

From the hallway came another two zombies, flailing at each other with fury, pushing to get into the room.

Zachary moved forward, swinging his gun and smashing the skull of the nearest zombie. The second one fell upon him before he could swing again. Zachary's head hit the cement floor with a hideous wet *crunch* while the enraged zombie ripped out his throat. I hoped the fall killed him, so he didn't feel the slow death of the zombie's bite. Either way, Zachary was gone. We'd been inside the walls of DC for maybe 10 minutes, and we'd already lost a man.

Zachary's death splintered our group instantly. It seemed like everyone was running in different directions, with zombies collapsing upon us from all sides. I had no time to get my bearings. Suddenly I realized Oliver was pulling me out a side door. "Wait! Celia!" I shouted, as we fell into another dim room and Oliver slammed the door shut. "Celia!"

From the other side of the door, I heard her muffled reply. "We'll find each other! Just be safe for now!" Then there was the loud *crack* of Ray's rifle and an inhuman shriek, then something thudded frantically against the door, shivering it in its frame. Oliver held it shut, shoulder against the wood, right hand clutching the knob, refusing to allow it to turn as he muttered something under his breath.

A second shot, slightly less loud. More feral sounds, and a door slamming. Some muffled yelling, one voice clearly Ray, the other Celia. Then the noise diminished, and for a long while Oliver sat with one ear pressed against the door, but neither of us could hear anything outside. The turmoil was replaced with eerie silence. And we waited.

After a time, Oliver turned the knob and opened the door a sliver. One of the zombies was lying dead against the other side, and as Oliver opened the door farther, its gore-covered remains fell into the room, spilling blood across the floor. The thing stank of rot and blood, and the uneasy smell of infection.

Oliver stepped over the body, peered into the room. Two more zombies were dead on the floor — the one Zachary brained, another presumably shot by Ray. In the middle of the room, Zachary himself lay dead, open eyes staring at the ceiling, like a man waiting for an angel from Heaven to come to his rescue. Uneasily, Oliver and I tiptoed past the bodies and into the hall.

"Where'd they go?" Oliver asked. He seemed on the verge of panic.

I tried to remain calm, but my worry for Celia was growing. "Let's just try to find them as quickly as possible, okay?" I said. Oliver nodded.

Without another word, he hurried off down the hall. "Hold on!" I called to his back. "We should look together!" But it was too late. Oliver turned a corner, moving quickly in his squat, waddling way, and was gone.

I stood alone in the hall, wondering what the hell to do. Wondering what the hell just happened. I chased after Oliver, but after a few turns, I had no idea if I was getting closer or farther away.

After some time, maybe eight or nine minutes, I heard Oliver cry out from down a long hallway. "This way! They're here!" I hurried to catch up to him, desperate to be sure that Celia was safe, barely thinking about Ray.

In the shrouded darkness of the building's interior, I found Oliver standing at the bottom of a stairwell that rose in stages toward an opening that shone bright with sunlight. He pointed to it, giving a strange little smile. "There." His eyes darted left and right, but that smile stayed. "They're up there! Through the door at the top of the stairs. They went up to get away from the zombies." He even made a little giggle, then caught himself and took the first step, turning back to gesture for me to follow.

We advanced up the stairs side by side, in silence. As we started the third and final flight before the top, I could feel Oliver looking over at me, and not for the first time I found myself wondering about this bizarre little man. This hermit whose home we'd invaded and whose life we'd turned upside-down. I wish I'd known him better. Maybe I would have seen it coming.

At the top of the stairs, I shielded my eyes against the blinding sunlight streaming through the open door. "Celia?" I asked excitedly, hoping for our group, what was left of it, to be reunited so we could keep going, do what we came for, and be gone. But mostly I just wanted to be sure she was all right. I stepped to the edge of the open door and, through squinted eyes, blinked and looked out. I didn't see Celia or Ray, or much of anything at all, for that matter.

And that's when Oliver pushed me from behind, and I fell, tumbling out into the bright, empty world.

15

I burst into the blinding light and fell like I'd been dropped from the sky, twisting toward my left side. I crashed to the pavement, *hard*, a snap and crack jolting through my left arm, air driven out of me. My small backpack absorbed some of the impact and probably saved me from even worse injuries, but it also forced me into an awkward lurch as I gasped and rolled, trying to find some angle where it didn't *hurt*. None existed. I knew right away that my left forearm was… *wrong*. Radius or ulna — maybe both — broken, possibly shattered beyond repair. My medical training leaped into my mind, but I tried not to think about the struggles of setting a complex fracture by myself, or the long, dubious recovery for someone my age.

I found myself on my back, looking up at the doorway. Outside its frame, tiny spurs of rusted orange metal were the only remnant of the landing and staircase that used to be there. The entire structure looked to have fallen in a heap of debris on the ground, where I'd missed landing on it by only a few feet. I suppose I could thank Oliver for at least pushing me out past the jutting metal that would have skewered me alive.

In the doorway, I saw him looking down at me through his round glasses. He pulled out a pistol I hadn't even realized he was carrying, and I steeled myself. Through gritted teeth, I said, "So now I meet the real Oliver." My left arm was propped close to my chest, like the broken wing of a bird.

For a long moment, Oliver didn't say anything. Finally, he snapped, "Why'd you have to show up, anyway? The clubhouse, that whole place, was mine, and everything was *fine*." He seemed like he had more to say, but it was lost in the voiceless rage that had bubbled to the surface. He sputtered and tried to speak, but eventually waved a hand, dismissing me in frustration. Then he raised his gun, sighting carefully, almost comically, down the barrel, until his eyes suddenly slid past me, saw something, then darted back. With a smirk, he slammed the metal gun against the rusty, open door three times, making a harsh, gong-like sound that echoed over the courtyard.

Behind me, I heard a grunt. Then another.

I was still spread out flat on the ground. Gingerly, I tilted my head up, giving myself an upside-down view of the space around me.

The courtyard was actually a dead-end alleyway, surrounded on three sides by the crumbling red-brick husks of connected buildings. Given the ruin of the exterior stairs, there was no escape except directly behind me, where the alleyway led out to an unknown street. And in that direction, something was moving.

Like a weasel returning to its den, Oliver slipped back into the doorway and was gone.

I rolled toward my right and struggled up onto my knees, trying to keep my left arm from touching the ground. But the arm slipped down with a flat, dead *thump*, accompanied by tiny crackling sounds that I felt deep inside, and I half-gasped, half-screamed at the pain. How many times in my previous life had I internally mocked some kid screaming and carrying on as I set his broken arm? I mentally apologized to any and all of those patients as I heaved myself to my feet and looked toward the alley entrance and whatever was out there.

My eyes focused on the movement, and my fears were confirmed. Two male zombies were skittering in my direction, investigating the sound Oliver had made. They didn't seem to have seen me yet — one benefit of the milky white eyes of the disease. But they were approaching and it wouldn't be long, especially given the fact that they were blocking my only way out. I looked from side to side, hoping for a miracle. I didn't see anything promising. In fact, I saw something less than promising.

Drawn by the sound, an infected dog, a German shepherd, I think, came into the alley and followed behind the two zombies shambling my way. The dog picked up its pace, thick, white froth falling from its pale tongue. Even from that distance — 50 yards or more — I began to make out the smell of the infected: fetid, rotting, filth, and disease. The humid mixture of sweat, blood, puss, urine, and feces, the worst combination of smells a living creature can produce.

I eased to my left, seeking the wall of the alley, maneuvering to protect my wounded side as I tried to find a place to hide or even mount a defense. There were a few steel trashcans overturned against the wall, and I slowly made my way to them, trying not to make quick movements or do anything else that might render me visible.

That was a mistake. In my haste, I'd forgotten about the dog's acute hearing, even given the ravages of the disease. It turned toward me as if I'd set off a flare gun. Padding more quickly, the dog passed the two zombies, moving straight toward me. I frantically scanned the alleyway for any sign of hope.

And I spotted my pistol on the pavement, just a few feet to my right. It must have slipped out of my waistband when I hit the ground.

The dog's sense of smell was another oversight. It now had a lock on me, and paused momentarily to prepare its attack. Its front legs formed a tense, inverted V as it let out a beastly, slathering growl. On either side of the dog, the two zombies continued forward, creating a three-pronged assault.

I thought to myself, *This is it.*

And I sprang for the gun.

Oh! The pain stabbed into my upper body, the jolt of another hard landing on the harsh pavement traveling through my cracked forearm. With my other arm, I reached out for the pistol, grabbed it, turned back toward my three attackers, fired.

The zombie on the left — dirty, green shirt, soiled khakis, thick work boots — took a hit to his left shoulder; the sound was like dropping a stone into thick mud. He spun backward, let out a garbled moan as he fell.

I knew I had to do better. I'd been aiming at the damn dog.

Who, even more incensed by the loud *bang* of the gun, leaped forward. I had only one more chance. At point-blank range, I fired again.

In a spray of blood and black-and-gray matted fur, a hole appeared in the dog's forehead, and he fell.

With no time to spare, I turned the gun toward the other approaching zombie, this one with the close-cropped haircut I remembered from the guards and military around DC. Based on the fact that his hair was still so short, I wondered if this was a relatively new one, recently turned. I pulled the trigger, and his left knee cap exploded. It was a debilitating injury, but *damn*, two bad shots. Like I had trained Celia, I'd been aiming for the gut, center of mass. He staggered and fell, tracing a long, slow arc toward my right. I tracked him on the way down, fired again, taking him through the center of his chest. He was dead when he hit the ground.

And suddenly I was facedown beside him, pain shooting up my arm. I yelled out, then bit down hard, clenching my teeth in an involuntary wince. The gun nearly flew from my grasp, but I held onto it like it was my last hope.

Which, I suppose, it was.

The other zombie had recovered from my first shot and was now on top of me, on my back, all snapping jaws, scratching, ragged fingernails, and violent thrashing. He tore into my backpack, but luckily not into me. I felt the grinding of bone on bone in my left arm as I jabbed backward with my right, launching my elbow into his side. The blow pushed him far enough to allow me to get the bulk of his weight off me. I turned over halfway. Furious, the zombie reared back on his knees, preparing for a final strike at my gut, one that would leave me flayed and dead in this unknown alleyway in DC. I rolled the rest of the way over onto my backpack, leaving my unprotected belly pointing toward the sky and the zombie.

As he lurched forward, I lifted the pistol to his forehead and squeezed the trigger.

The only sound was a dry *click*. Empty.

Now it was the zombie's turn. He ignored my useless gun, tore into my chest with his teeth and fingernails. And I *screamed*. I *screamed*. I *screamed*. No words, no language, just the incomprehensible sounds of unbridled pain. Every muscle tensed. Every nerve ending alive. By reflex more than anything else, I used my good hand, the one still holding the gun, to punch at his head. In my frenzy, the butt of the pistol became a hammer, and I turned into the embodiment of fury, slam, *slam*, *SLAM*, *SLAM*, *SLAM*, *SLAM*. Then there was a new sound. A wet, gooey *SPLAT*. The zombie rolled off me, dead.

All I wanted to do was catch my breath. Catch my breath. I couldn't. It was too hard. I tried, I tried, but it was too hard. I dropped the pistol, touched my chest, found torn skin and blood, too much blood. My breathing wouldn't slow down. There wasn't enough air in the alleyway, not enough air in the world, how was I supposed to breathe? I panted, gasped. A vague thought in the back of my mind said to fight it, to calm down, but I couldn't. I tore my shirt open, trying to get more air, even though the winter day was so cold.

And the world fell away, nothing left, no sky, no sun, no light, no cold, no alleyway, no zombie, no blood. No air. *No air.*

16

Black.

Everything was black.

Through a thick, sleepy fog, I turned my head, opened my eyes, but the blackness was complete. I couldn't see a thing, not in any direction. *Where the hell am I?* It was my only coherent thought.

In time, I faded out again. To black.

* * *

Then the world was grey. Differing shades, from light to dark. A sense that it was morning.

I opened my eyes again.

I was in a room, a large room, institutional ceiling tile overhead, moldy and water-stained, in repeating rectangles. There were light fixtures up there, too, but none were on. And, almost directly above me, a small circle of light-colored plastic.

Was that a smoke alarm? My God. Had the whole thing been a dream? A decade of disease and death, just a figment of my imagination? A smoke alarm. Such a mundane thing, so commonplace, and yet it'd had no place in the universe I'd dreamed up, the world of RL2013.

I raised my head as much as I could, until my chin nearly touched my chest, and looked around. I was in a hospital, lying on a bed, with white sheets covering my body. Maybe I'd had some sort of episode, maybe I'd been in a coma. That might explain how my mind had turned in on itself, and fabricated all of it. Ten years of an imaginary plague. I grinned, a stupid grin, a sheepish grin. I felt like a fool, and like the luckiest man in the world. The dream was over, and everything was back to normal.

My chest *itched.*

I went to scratch it, but my hand, the left one, felt like it weighed a ton. How strange. Straining with extra effort, I tried to raise my left arm. And I couldn't. I tried my right arm. Nothing.

Not because my arms were too heavy. But because they were strapped down.

Okay, I thought. *Maybe they didn't want me flailing or rolling out of bed. That's understandable.*

I heard a creak, and a thin shaft of light broke across the room. Footsteps.

Tilting my head, I saw a low, squat woman in a dark grey dress amble into the room, toward a table in the far corner. She walked quietly, not talking to me or even looking in my direction.

"Hey —" I tried to speak, but my voice was dry and cracking, barely audible. I licked my lips and swallowed, trying again. "Hey. You there."

The woman stopped in her tracks and turned in my direction. After a brief look through squinting, calculating eyes, she turned back toward the door. "James, I'm going to need you in here," she said. Her voice was craggy with a lilting uptick, some sort of brogue, but if she'd ever had a true accent, it had mostly faded. She was short and thick, with curls of grey hair that only hinted at their former brown.

From outside, a deep voice replied. "Yes, ma'am." The sliver of light grew and a shadow stepped through it. A large, dark-skinned man in green fatigues, walking toward her in long, purposeful strides. The room remained dim, but the light from the open door was enough to see clearly. The man, James, made no effort to hide the pistol on his right hip, or the hand that rested on its handle, ready. When he reached the old woman, he turned toward me and stopped.

The woman came closer.

"What's going on here?" I started in a slow, tired voice. "How long have I — ", She grabbed at my chin, opening my mouth and looking inside. Then she turned my head from side to side, peering at me in a curious way. I figured she was my nurse, though I was far from impressed by her bedside manner. Her hand left my chin, and she pulled down the white sheets, revealing large wraps of bandages across my chest. *I must have had some kind of accident*, I thought, still in a fog. The woman reached across to prod my left arm, checking it. With the sheet pulled down, I saw a cast — a sloppy, makeshift job, in my opinion — covering my forearm. *Was I in a car accident or something?* And I saw the straps, holding me tight.

I looked up at the woman, studying her for a second or two, blinking my eyes to try to clear my head. I noticed smudges of grease on her forehead. Her fingernails were ragged, dirty. In my daze, I asked the first thing that came to mind. "Shouldn't you wash up before seeing a patient?"

She pulled up, eyes wide, forehead wrinkled in surprise. She mocked me with a tiny bow, her hint of brogue blooming into a full-on Irish accent. "So sorry, your highness," she sneered. "Please accept me deepest apologies. I'll submit me resignation and be gone in the morning. In the meantime, can I get you a pair of fluffy slippers, or perhaps a cup o' tea?" She huffed and walked toward the door.

"Wait!" I pleaded, but she didn't turn.

To James, she said, back in her normal voice, "Well, I guess it's true then. Hell, I guess it's *all* true."

"Isn't that a *good* thing?" James asked.

She stood, head down, then turned to look back at me. "It is. And thank the good Lord, if He's still paying attention." She stepped quickly out of the room, followed by James, and the door closed behind them, punctuated with a loud click.

* * *

Hours passed, and I drifted off to sleep again. I'd tried shouting after them, but to no avail. No one came.

Finally, I awoke to the creak of the door. The old woman and James stepped into the room and just stared at me.

I turned my head toward them, unable to do anything else. "Can't you at least tell me what's going on?" I slowly shook my head, trying to chase away the butterflies clouding my thoughts.

She shook her head. "I can't."

"Who are you, at least?"

She shrugged. "My name's Hilde, not that I matter a whit. But there is someone who wants to see you." She regarded me skeptically. "Do you think you can walk? I don't have a wheelchair, your majesty."

I winced and shook my head. "Look, I'm sorry about earlier. I just don't know where I am. Or how I got here. Was I in a coma? I had this terrible dream."

She considered what I said with a wry look. "Terrible dream, indeed. You've been out a few days, mostly because I kept you knocked out. Better for you. It took a lot of my drugs, and I hope they weren't wasted on you." She tilted her head, set her mouth. I couldn't tell what she was thinking about me, only that it was… *complicated.* My mind still foggy, I couldn't understand everything. *Why was this nurse skeptical of me? Why was I under armed guard?* And more than anything, looking up at the dim ceiling, *why were the lights still off?*

Turning to the man next to her, Hilde said, "Come on, James, let's try to get him up."

17

We stepped out into the hallway. And there, any sense of my past 10 years being a dream shattered. RL2013 was real, not a fantasy. Not a coma-induced hallucination. On either side of the hall, filthy children and adults huddled, watching me stagger past, half-carried by James and Hilde. This wasn't a hospital from days gone by, with pristine walls and gleaming floors, and guidelines on everything from sanitary procedures to visiting hours. This was *now*. And *here*. A time and a world where simply having a place like this to recuperate was a luxury. Although I was thankful for what these people had given me — a place, a way to recover — I'm sure I couldn't hide the disappointment in my eyes.

My legs were unsteady, untrustworthy from days of disuse. James and Hilde continued to help me along as we made our way down unknown corridors and halls.

I was uncovered and untethered. My pants and shoes had been left alone, thankfully, but my shirt was gone, exposing my bandaged chest and my left arm, now encased in a makeshift cast. The people in the halls ogled. Men, women, children, they all stared. I suppose I would have, too, seeing this old grey beast walk by, held together by spit and glue.

A young boy, maybe 12, stepped in front of me suddenly, reached out a hand, touched my good arm. "Now there are three," he said in a wistful sort of voice, before James pushed him gently but firmly out of the way. As the kid ran off down a connecting hall, he said it again, louder. "Now there are three!" More faces turned to look at me.

Three? Three what?

"What does that mean?" I asked Hilde.

The three of us paused, and Hilde stared at me with knowledge behind her eyes. But it was knowledge she wasn't willing to share. "I already told you, I don't matter a whit," she said. "And I like it that way. Keeping to myself, doing my job, it keeps me out of trouble, and it keeps trouble away from me. Far as I am concerned, you're someone else's problem now. I want to go back to my simple routine. If you have questions, you're going to need to ask someone more important than me."

Hilde nodded to James, and they started up again, directing me down one hall, turning, down another, through a doorway. I became tired, feet beginning to drag.

"Come on, old-timer. It's not far now," James said, more kindly than I would have expected. Helping me walk, he guided me through another door and into a room crowded with people, all of them standing. We pushed our way into the middle of the room, where I was relieved to find a chair, blocky and cushioned, with squat legs, probably borrowed from a waiting room, assuming the building used to be a hospital. I sat down heavily.

The crowd parted and settled, finding places to stand along each wall, or sitting on the floor. It seemed clear from the way people were inspecting their fingernails or idly running their hands through their hair that they were waiting for something.

Finally, when I was nearly ready to doze off in the chair, I heard someone enter from a door behind me. Footsteps crossed the room, and the murmur of the crowd died off.

The chair was too big to slide around, and I was too tired to get up. I waited for whoever had entered to come to me.

"Good, you're awake."

That voice. *That voice.* It was…

"Hank?" I asked, craning my neck to see the person behind me.

"And me," a woman's voice said, and she stepped into view, her braided hair falling across one side of her denim shirt. The man joined her in front of me, like the reveal at the end of an incredible magic trick.

Hank and Janine. From The Oasis.

"I don't believe it," was all I could manage. I sagged back into the chair and squinted up at them, amazed, my jaw hanging open like I was trying to catch flies.

18

I'd only just come to terms with the fact that I hadn't created the whole outbreak in a dream. And now, here were Hank and Janine, ghosts from my past, threatening to once more upend my reality.

Hank and Janine, the very same scouts from The Oasis who first guided Rosa and me to the supplies she needed to mass-produce the cure. And who later accidentally led the hordes from Atlanta back to the camp, resulting in its downfall and destruction.

"What're you *doing here?*" I finally asked.

Hank chuckled and shrugged. "We have some shortwave radios around that still work, and I hear there's a new Oasis. In Maryland. You have anything to do with that?" Now it was my turn to shrug. *Perhaps.* I wasn't ready to tell everything just yet. It was all too confusing.

So they told me their story. Part of it, I already knew, because I'd lived it, too. The attack on The Oasis. The mayhem, the rush and struggle to break free.

After that, Janine said, they just *guessed*. They knew that Rosa and I were from DC, and they'd seen our RV's mad-dash escape. With Atlanta gone, they correctly guessed that we might try to take the cure to DC. After all, it was nominally in charge of what was left of the country.

They couldn't escape from the besieged, burning Oasis by car, but were able to run though the surrounding dark woods to freedom. They made it out with their ready-packs, loaded with supplies they always had available for scouting runs, and one gun each. For weeks, they hiked on side roads, avoiding highways in case anyone from Atlanta continued north from The Oasis. They scrounged any food, water, and supplies they could find. The fact that they were traveling as a pair saved them. Countless times, one of them found water where the other had seen nothing, or fended off a random zombie attack the other had stepped into. As they told their tale, finishing one another's sentences, sharing private looks, it dawned on me that Hank and Janine were more than just business partners.

Somewhere in Virginia, they chanced upon two bicycles with flat tires. After only a day, the struggle of pedaling with the floppy, deflated tires was too much, and they abandoned the bikes by the side of the road. They walked the rest of the way to DC.

By the time they reached the city's walls, Rosa's message had done its tragic work. The government had been overthrown. People rebelled, not only against their totalitarian rulers, but against each other. Fighting had broken out all over the city. Thousands had died. The chaos lasted for months. Those who were left clung together in pockets. After a time staying across the river in Virginia, Hank and Janine slipped easily into the unguarded city. And then, living in the city, they joined forces with some of the survivors.

As they related the story, I could barely hold back my anguish. Janine put a hand on my shoulder. "We heard about what Rosa said, and what happened to her," she said softly. "It's pretty much a legend among the people who are left here. You couldn't have known what was going to happen, how everyone would react. But those of us that remained… since then, people like us have been looking everywhere. We've been looking for *you*."

"You said *thousands* died!" I could feel the tears, and didn't try to stop them. "*That's* our legacy. We came here to offer hope and a new chance. But what we really offered was *death*." I buried my head in my hands. Through my palms, I choked out the words: "These people would have been better off keeping the damn government, and never knowing about the cure."

There was silence. Neither Janine nor Hank had a rebuttal for that. They just looked at me, with sympathy that burned like scorn.

An earnest young man stepped forward, maybe 18 or 19, with a shock of dirty blond hair drooping down over a face that was just showing signs of beard stubble. "No," he said. He stopped himself, looked at Janine and Hank like he was weighing the political consequences of interrupting them, but decided he wanted to talk anyway. "No, we wouldn't be better off. Look, people decided to fight each other, no one can change that. But what you told us was that *there's a chance*. There's a reason to have hope. That means more to us than the walls and the security and everything else. We lived like prisoners. Every choice was made for us. Now, we're *free*." He swept his hands around at all the others sitting on the floor and lining the walls, and I saw nods of agreement. "Sure, we struggle, but it's *our struggle*. It's our choice to make, not just some assignment to keep us placated. And now that you're here, there's *three* of you. That alone is incredible." He looked from me to Hank to Janine. *There are three*. Of course. That's what the kid in the hall had meant. *Now there are three people with the cure*. "Plus, it's *you*," he said. "From across the river, from the day we learned the truth. And you...." He trailed off, suddenly unsure of himself, and Hank stepped forward.

"Everyone here knows about us," Hank said, gesturing to himself and Janine. "And they all know about you. Only a few people heard Rosa in person, but the story spread like wildfire. I daresay some of the folks here could recite what she said that day word for word." A low murmur spread through the crowd. "They know we're unique — Janine, you, and me, the only people left who were cured by the fabled Oasis." The murmur grew with anticipation, a sound almost like reverence. Hank's face was a tangled knot of hope, concern, excitement, utter fear. "Do you still have *it*? Do you have the eggs? *The cure?*"

The crowd didn't move, didn't whisper. Every breath was held waiting for my answer.

How long ago had Rosa and I stood overlooking this city? How long had it been since she spoke the words that ended her life, and ripped these people's world apart? Months? More than a year. How much more? Now, I was about to shatter every one of their remaining hopes.

"No," I said.

Hank's face dropped. Janine turned away. The crowd erupted in shouts and wails. People either argued with each other or consoled one another, or both.

In one corner, I saw her.

A little girl, 4 or 5 by my estimation, sitting cross-legged by herself. All she did was look at me. Her eyes were like those of a dead animal, staring, seeing nothing. A girl who should have embodied the innocence of her youth, the joy of simply being a child, instead looked shell-shocked and hollow. Those empty eyes glistened for a moment, then tears began to stream down her cheeks. Her hands clutched at a dirty, fuzzy shape in her lap, a beloved toy or blanket, something to give her comfort. Still, her gaze remained locked on me.

I felt like I was suffocating. It was too much to bear, the hopes and dreams of every other living soul. But I'd come here for a reason, and seeing the dead-faced little girl in front of me, that reason came slamming back into my mind like a door closing, shutting out my own despair, blasting away all the cobwebs of indecision and fear.

I pushed myself up out of the chair, held up my right hand. "But," I said.

The crowd was too loud, too absorbed in their own anger and misery. I cleared my throat and spoke again, much louder, with all the force I could muster. "But —"

People in the crowd turned in surprise. Janine heard me and began waving her hands to quiet people down. "Let him talk!" she yelled.

As the group slowly grew silent, I waited until everyone's eyes were on me again. "But there is still hope." People looked confused, overwhelmed, accusatory. I kept talking. "I don't have the eggs, and I can't just give you the cure. But I *have* given it to someone else. A woman, a friend. Her name is Celia, and I've cured her, too. With my blood. And I know there's a way to get it out, for the rest of you. I came here to look for the right people — people Rosa would've worked with before the government collapsed. People who can take what's inside me — inside Hank, and Janine, too — and get it out. Replicate it. Give it to all of you."

Scanning the room again, I could see a strange look on people's faces. *I had cured someone else.* They seemed dumbstruck, like they didn't know what to believe anymore. I couldn't blame them. "You tell me that you struggled, and that the struggle was worth it," I said. "And maybe a lot of that struggle was to find me. Well, I'm here now. But I'm not the *end* of the struggle. It's time for all of us to struggle together. To find the people I need, to end this damned disease forever." As I spoke, my voice gained momentum, volume. My last words rang out as a shout in the crowded room.

Everyone stayed quiet. Then the young man, the one who'd interrupted us just moments before, came over and embraced me. A few other people did, too, and finally, the little girl with the lifeless eyes got up off the floor and held out her arms to me.

My God, I thought. *What have I done?*

19

"That's across the divide," Hank said, sounding concerned.

"The divide?" I raised an eyebrow. The room had been cleared, leaving only Janine, Hank, and me. I told them my plan, what little there was. My first thought was to go to the NIH branch nearby — the lab, the place Rosa used to work — hoping it was still there, with people who could run the machines we'd need to manufacture the cure. It was a pretty ambitious hope.

Then, as Janine unconsciously twirled her long, braided hair, she told me how I'd come to be in this room, whatever and wherever it was. After the organized fighting in the city had died down, gunshots were relatively rare, so when one of their scouts heard shots fired, he naturally went to see what was going on. Luckily for me, that scout stumbled across the dead-end alley where I was lying unconscious, surrounded by two dead zombie humans and a dead zombie dog. He

had no idea who I was, but Hank had also been scouting nearby —
never one to pass his duties along to someone else, even though he
was in charge now. Although he had to look past my longer hair and
scraggly beard, Hank recognized me, and with the other scout,
dragged me to get help.

They'd taken me to this old hospital, formerly called Providence
Hospital, in the northeast quadrant of the city. It served as their
headquarters — part home, part sick bay, part operations control. It
probably hadn't been all that new when the outbreak happened, and
the ensuing decade had only added mold, dust, and the crumbling
detritus of decay to its already bland, boxy appearance. The damp
scent of mildew filled every breath, and I felt my old, ingrained fear
of dirt and filth crop up, illogical as it was.

They asked me how in the hell I ended up half-dead in that alley.
I told them about my mission to spread the cure, and with something
very close to hatred, I spoke about Oliver. I paused, trying to regain
my composure.

I told them I was I wanted to go to the NIH branch lab on
Capitol Hill, the facility near my old home where Rosa had worked.
But they dissuaded me, telling me that their scouts had been all
through that area. The only people left were a few pockets of
survivors that shunned their attempts to connect. And, of course, the

zombies. So I changed the plan, and decided that we needed go to the main NIH campus instead.

"The divide," Janine said, digging out an old stubby pencil. "It cuts the city in half, basically. North-south. Do you remember the layout of the city?"

I nodded. "I think so. Maybe even better than you, given that I lived around here... *before*."

"Well, fine, but a lot of what you remember has changed." She began to draw, right on the surface of the table in front of us. "DC is shaped like a diamond — half of one, really — but the walls weren't built around the whole thing. Mostly, they protect the government buildings — here, from the river, through the middle of the city, and up to the north a bit." She drew an irregular shape outlining where the walls stood. "Anywhere the density of the buildings and population dropped off, it must not have been worth it to make walls. Or maybe someone was just playing favorites. Anyway, a lot of this up here —" she pointed to the northeast section "— isn't inside the walls, and they stop on the west around here, too." Her pencil tip hovered over an area just west of the city center. "Then, they made another pocket over here, so there's a whole different set of walls that enclose this area." She drew a crude oval over the western portion of the diamond. "There used to be a connector between the two walled sections, before the fighting, but it didn't take long for the government to destroy that. Now the two parts are completely separate."

"That middle portion, in between the two walled areas — what you're calling 'the divide' — it's... Rock Creek Park?" My mind forced up these ancient memories.

"Yeah, that's it," Janine said. "Well, it used to be a park. Over time, the woods have become much more dense, but it's probably the best source of fresh water around. So, like you might expect, it draws a lot of *animals*. Animals of all kinds. Including zombies. *Lots* of zombies." Janine tapped her pencil on the open space in the drawing to make her point.

Hank jumped in. "So, what's she's saying is, if you want to go to NIH, you gotta go through there."

"We couldn't, you know, go around or something?" I asked.

Shaking his head, Hank said, "Nah, not really. To the south, it connects to the Potomac. And it runs pretty far north. You could go around it that way, to the north, but that'd be much more dangerous than just going through it. The shortest path is near the middle, where the two walls are closest together." He paused, letting me think about it. "And one more problem. Once the government pulled out of the city, that's the direction they went. And they blew up the bridges on the way out. The only way across the divide is literally to cross the river. We'll need to get our feet wet."

I sighed deeply. *Can nothing be easy?* Then I thought about the Bay Bridge, and those zombies on the other bridge that forced us south. "Okay, fine," I said. "Maybe I'm sick of bridges, anyway. When can we go?"

* * *

To say they babied me would be overstating things, but not by much. More than six weeks passed before Hank would agree to let me go. In that time, I saw how they lived, holed up in this old hospital, sleeping on floors, using anything they could find to make a "normal" life. Old privacy curtains became walls. The undersides of desks became bedrooms.

I thought of Celia a lot. I asked Hank to send people out to look for her, and he did, but they didn't find her. Or Ray. Or even Oliver. I hoped against hope that she had made it to safety, back the The Oasis. I wanted to go back, to make sure she was okay. But I also needed to push on, to seek the cure. Then I could go back, bringing something they really needed. If Oliver was there, I'd deal with him. Of that I was sure.

But first, I had to suffer through the tedious weeks of recovery. I spent a lot of time learning how they lived, if only to take up the time.

Keeping on top of the food and water supply was hard, but manageable. DC had been stocked for a larger population, and now that the numbers were much smaller, it was possible to make do. Even my old FDC on Capitol Hill was found to be rather well-supplied with food, tucked into secure rooms in the basement, and every bit of it was brought back to the hospital.

Janine and Hank's group was even rather ingenious about their method of managing the other half of the food-consumption process: waste removal. A large section of the third floor on the east end of the building was converted into a series of stalls that opened to the outdoors via holes. People could go in, do their business, and have it drop to the ground stories below. No one had to risk disease by fouling their living space, or risk attack by going outside. A crew of people had the unsavory job of shoveling, tilling, and burying the waste at intervals, but it worked. Hank told me the idea came from medieval castles, from a history buff in the group. Up on the third floor, on days when there was a breeze, you could hardly smell it. Well, that's a lie. But you could smell it a lot *less*.

I talked to as many people as possible, asking a lot of questions. On one occasion, I sat with James, the same man who had guarded over me when I first arrived. We talked about life in this DC. I asked where the other people were. Pointing out a window, across the city, he replied. "They're out there, all over. We've asked people to join up, but everyone seems happy to stay where they are for now. Over there," he said, gesturing north and east, "there's a pretty big group. They've got a lot of firepower, so we keep an eye on 'em. Their leader, a guy named Duke, seems like a decent fellow. But he doesn't trust us enough to join up."

When six weeks were up, I was so ready, I could taste it. My chest was still heavily scabbed from where the zombie had gouged it, and my left forearm, while free from its cast, felt weak, tentative. But I didn't care. My life during recovery was relatively comfortable, but had been reduced to a boring repetition of mundane daily tasks. And on top of that, I'd felt their eyes. Every day, wherever I went, they were on me. Eyes of expectation, and hope. Eyes that, as days passed, started to *demand* something from me. To implore me to do something.

When it finally came time to make preparations for the trip to NIH, we had to decide on a team. The journey involved significant risk of zombie attack, so it made sense that Hank, Janine, and I would go — a bite to us wasn't a death sentence. Many of the others opposed this, saying it was too risky to have all the leaders gone at once, but Hank and Janine brushed aside their concern. As for me, I didn't see how I could be even considered one of their leaders, so I didn't say anything.

* * *

We set out on a cool, overcast morning, as winter was giving way but spring still felt remote. Each of us had a supply pack and a pistol. As we headed west toward the divide, Janine carried a folding map of DC, so old that not even RL2013 could be blamed for its demise. Having been almost completely replaced by GPS years before the outbreak, we were fortunate to have the old paper dinosaur as a reference. A sudden gust of wind kicked up, so Janine carefully folded the map's vertical rectangles to show only the section of the city we needed. One long flap in the back caught the wind and tore loose with only the faintest rustle. "Damn," Janine muttered, pulling the pieces back together.

The route west took several zigs and zags, each of which Janine confirmed with her map. As we walked, I couldn't help but stare. DC had been my home for 10 years, but this part of the city was as alien to me as another world. For reasons I couldn't explain, a larger road marked as Georgia Avenue was divided down the middle by a row of parked cars and trucks — from the smallest coupes to minivans and even box trucks — that stretched as far as I could see in either direction. Some of the vehicles were burnt and hollow, blackened husks left to decay on the crumbling pavement. Others looked like you could start them up and drive away. Was this some sort of defense? If so, from what? And yet, beyond this makeshift barricade, some things were familiar, or cut from the same cloth as my old life. We passed this neighborhood's Food Dispersal Center, and the very name reminded me of the day I met Rosa. But unlike the large brick building I was familiar with on Capitol Hill, this FDC was split into two parts — small markets across the street from each other, with signs denoting them as Petworth FDC 1 and 2.

A short section of fence stood in front of Petworth FDC 2, and from somewhere behind it, we heard a noise. The sound of someone or something rummaging though trash. We all froze. Hank made the completely unnecessary universal gesture to be quiet, holding his right index finger up to his lips. Then he pointed the same finger down the road, in the direction we'd been traveling. *Let's just keep going, quietly.* That was the most obvious solution, so we did.

But it wasn't going to be that easy for us. The wind blew hard, and again Janine's paper map caught it, snapping with loud *fwap*, just for a second, then tearing apart. As Janine reached for the section that was about to blow away, she let out an involuntary gasping sound. *Hmph!*

From the fence, a ragged woman stood up straight and looked right at us, long, blonde hair clumped and greasy with neglect. Instantly, a rage took over her face, and she snapped her jaws at us, making a slathering sound. She lunged at the fence, but it stopped her, and for a brief moment she didn't know how get to us. Then, shaking her head, with what little consciousness remained, she shoved herself away from the fence, staggered to the side.

Hank took advantage of the zombie's momentary confusion, stepped up to the fence, and deftly planted a tool that looked like a combination hammer and ax into her right temple. She let out a hideous shriek as the blunt metal weapon ended her life with a sickening wet crunch.

"Hank — " Janine started. He didn't look up, wiping the mess off his hammer. "Hank!" she said, more urgently, and he snapped his head around. Janine was pointing to an alley that joined the street ahead of our path. There, three more zombies stumbled out from behind a low brick wall. Drawn by the commotion, they stepped toward us.

"Ah, damn," Hank sighed. "We haven't even reached the divide yet. I didn't expect all this trouble so soon."

"What do we do?" I asked.

"Fight or run," he replied.

"Run? How far is it?"

Hank looked to Janine, who glanced at her map. The zombies ambled closer, the one in front desperately trying to see through milky eyes, to find out what these strange noises were.

"To the divide?" Janine said. "Six or seven blocks — *long* blocks."

"You two have any idea how old I am?" I wasn't liking the sound of either option.

Hank nodded to Janine. "Then we fight. Kill these three, quiet as possible." The two of them set to work. The zombies, as they approached, became enraged, sensing prey or danger. I pulled out my pistol, aiming it at the closest one, thinking to myself, *I'm going to shoot someone by mistake.* Hank brained the lead zombie as it leaped toward him, filthy hands raised like claws. Then he looked back, waved a hand at me. "Put that away!" he hissed. "Too much noise!" Janine, her map tucked away, had produced a hammer tool like Hank's and shattered a zombie's kneecap with a quick, hard strike. As the thing fell and started to wail and snap, she hit it a second time, a fatal blow to the head. The third zombie rushed in and got a hand on Janine before she could pull back her hammer, but Hank was there, and it died from a single, brutal shot that smashed in its face. It fell away from Janine in a lump.

Moving with surgical economy, Janine and Hank scanned the surrounding area as they wiped down their tools and tucked them away. Janine pulled the map out again, pointed down the street, whispered, "This way. Come on." We walked as quickly and quietly as we could, toward the divide.

20

The wall followed the north-south line of 16th Street, but was far from secure. It had been battered and broken, with whole sections fallen into the street in ruins. In this part of DC, the wall was metal and brick and block — anything they could cobble together to make a run so many miles long, it seemed. Whether the broken sections marked places where people tried to get out or where something tried to get in, it was impossible to tell.

We stepped over piles of brick and through a large rift, and suddenly we were standing in the place they called the divide.

At first, the city looked much the same — rowhouses fanned out down side streets. But the houses were long abandoned, roofs collapsed, windows gone, porches caved in. The natural world was slowly reclaiming its land, with weeds and long grasses growing everywhere. Bushes, saplings, and trees sprouted all around, filling huge cracks in the pavement, and pushing up through the center of some homes that were no longer enclosed by four walls. What used to be a tree-lined street was now much less of a street and more like a forest.

I realized with surprise that it smelled different. It smelled *better*. Where the city had always carried the lingering scent of decay, trash, even death, the divide smelled like *nature*. Like life. I took a deep breath.

Within a few more blocks, the empty rowhouses gave way to empty single-family homes, some of them large and stately. *I wonder what that place must have sold for*, I thought to myself as we passed a huge Victorian with a wraparound porch, chuckling a bit until I considered how long it had been since the idea of *money* had even crossed my mind, then guffawing out loud. Janine looked at me with a sidelong glance, but didn't ask what was so amusing.

As the day wore on and our journey continued, the trees grew denser. The sun was muted behind thick clouds. We walked a long, slow, downward route, knowing there was a river somewhere in front of us. Finally, we approached a bend in the road and saw it. To our right, the remains of a bridge had fallen in crumbles of concrete and rebar into the river, neatly severed on both sides by what I guessed was some sort of explosion. Just like the Navy had done in Annapolis.

We stepped over a rusted guard rail and shuffled down to the water's edge. The river looked chilly and swollen, probably from an early spring thaw upstream. Hank was the first one to the bank, and he turned and looked back at me. "It's going to be really cold," he said, "but I don't think it's too deep here. Besides, we can use a lot of this debris like stepping stones." He gestured to the fallen bits of the bridge. "Be careful and be quiet. We haven't seen anything here yet, but that doesn't mean it's safe."

As if on cue, a raccoon emerged from the woods on the other side of the river. Although it was some distance away, I thought from the look of it that it was infected. It drank some water from the river, then hobbled off along the bank and disappeared. Hank stepped down into the water, and we followed.

Within a few steps, Hank gingerly toed himself onto a slab of concrete, leaving wet footprints. With a delicate leap, he jumped to the next slab. Janine followed his lead.

Damn, it's cold, I thought as my feet touched the water. I quickly hopped onto the first concrete steppingstone, now wet with dripping footprints. Hank was maybe a dozen feet ahead, pulling himself up onto another block of concrete, and Janine was dropping down into the water just behind him. I positioned myself to make the little jump to the second block — and saw something move out of the corner of my eye.

In mid jump, I turned my head to the left and saw them. More than a dozen zombies wading through the shallow waters. Like the one I'd seen so long ago by my dock on the Eastern Shore, I thought, *Are they fishing?*

And I fell.

My foot hit the second concrete slab and slipped on its slick surface. The hard slab rushed upward, slamming into my hip, scraping against my ribs. The air was knocked out of me in a loud *whoosh* as my legs splashed loudly into the water. For a moment, I felt dizzy, like I might faint. Then the cold rushing waters surrounded me and I thought that I might even drown. But violent hands grabbed me, and when I snapped out of it Hank and Janine were lifting me to my feet. "Move!" Hank shouted, inches from my face. "Come on! Now!" Hoisting my arms over their shoulders, he and Janine mostly carried me through the frigid waters.

My head lolled, my eyes blinked, trying to find focus. When I had regained my breath, the world around me wasn't quite so fuzzy, and I saw them. All of them. Streaming toward us on both sides, sloshing through the river. Dozens of zombies. A sound like the buzzing of bees filled my ears, but louder. An inhuman collection of grunts, snarls, growls, as the swarm approached us, from left and right.

Hank and Janine ran through the water, flat out dragging me with them, no longer making any attempt to be quiet, only trying to get away. I wanted to help, but my legs felt like they belonged to someone else. I paddled my feet in the water like an infant learning to swim, without power or purpose. "Up here!" Hank said, guiding us up the tiny incline on the far side of the river. We slipped in the mud, almost fell. The closest zombies were so near I began to smell their fetid reek. Then my mind exploded with a sound too sudden to bear. My ears rang, my vision flashed. Janine had fired her pistol toward the left, dropping a zombie dead into the water. Two more leaped on top of it, snapping and tearing, aimlessly raging.

Hank pulled me up the slope. "You've gotta help us, or you're dead." His eyes were wide, serious.

I shook my head once, twice. " Okay," was all I could say. I put weight on my legs, they held. I took a step, with Janine still supporting me. "Okay." I nodded. It was the most sincere gesture I could manage.

Another blast, and another, as both Hank and Janine shot at the approaching zombies. Panning my head in a slow circle, I saw them in tattered groups off into the distance. The gunfire was drawing more of them. More than I'd ever seen in one place before. The reality of it sapped my will, my ability to think straight, to even hope we had a chance.

Janine grabbed my arm and Hank pushed me forward. We tumbled along a two-lane street and into the woods, with a line of zombies trailing behind, tracking us in their animal way. Hank took us in among the trees, hoping for cover. We found an iron fence and followed it, until we discovered a missing section and stepped through to the other side. Hank used several fallen branches to block the gap in the fence, and we kept moving.

Just behind us, the zombies hit the fence, lashed at it, lacking the simple logic to aim for the open section. But there were so many. *So many.* Several of them found the gap by sheer accident, falling over the branches and through. Others followed, and they continued to chase us, as Hank dragged us farther and farther into the deep woods.

Then, all at once, decaying houses stood before us, first single-family homes, then rowhouses, the reverse of what we'd encountered on the other side. We were through the divide. Janine pulled out her map, tried to study it as we pushed west on crumbling streets, a pack of zombies still tracking us. My focus returned, or at least a sense of self-preservation, and I forced myself to press on. But I was tired, and sore. And old. I felt so very old. Hank guided us in arbitrary circles, looping around houses, trying to lose any of the zombies still hunting us.

"Rest," I gasped, falling backward into the brick wall of one of the houses. Hank nodded, held a finger to his lips. *Shhh.* He peered around the side of the wall.

After a time, I caught my breath, although breathing remained difficult. I suspected a broken rib or two. Maybe cracked my hip up, too. Janine was absorbed in the map, looking for nearby street signs. When Hank finally gestured that all was clear, we gathered around Janine.

"We're *here*," she said, tapping on the west side of the green swath labeled Rock Creek Park. Then she dragged her finger up and to the left, to a grey blob beside one of the larger roads. "And this is where we need to go."

"Then let's go," I said, trying to use a businesslike demeanor to hide the pain I was in. Hank just nodded, and we set off.

Quietly, cautiously, we made our way north and west. At last, we stepped onto a wide, six-lane boulevard marked as Wisconsin Avenue. Janine pointed north. "NIH is just up the road here," she said.

* * *

It took hours of laborious, deliberate walking for me to make the journey. Hank and Janine were equal parts patient and restless, wanting to push ahead faster, but knowing I couldn't.

At last, we found what we were looking for. A large metal wall blocked the road, encircling a wide campus of buildings on our left and right. From Janine's map, we knew that the National Institutes of Health were here, just ahead of where we were standing. A solid, closed gate barred the way.

Hank approached the gate. Remembering other encounters at other walls, I was certain that at any moment he would be gunned down. But nothing happened.

Hank disappeared, following the wall around a bend and out of view, trying to find a way in. A few minutes later, the gate in front of us slid open, and we saw Hank looking out at us from inside. Gesturing for us to follow, he strolled into the compound. I closed the gate behind us as we continued north.

After a time, we spotted a series of large, uniform signs telling us we were in the right place, and we approached a glass and brick building. With a sinking feeling, I saw that several windows had been broken in. We climbed in one and made our way down a darkened hallway.

Then Janine stopped. "Do you hear that?" she asked.

We paused, listened. There was a very low hum coming from somewhere up ahead. We crept forward, tracking the sound, trying to bring it closer. Slowly, slowly, it got louder.

As we turned a corner, we heard something else: voices. A hurried conversation. My heart raced. We were here. *They* were here. Could it be? Just ahead, the hallway ended in a set of closed double doors, and from between them, a tiny sliver of light escaped. In an instant, that light vanished, accompanied by scraping noises and a loud click. In the sudden darkness, I noticed a red light high on the wall, and guessed it was a surveillance camera. They'd seen us coming, at least once we entered the hallway. Behind the doors, it sounded like someone was making a shushing sound, telling someone else to be quiet.

We approached the door, and Hank tried to push it open. On the other side, a chain rattled. Locked, maybe reinforced. We heard a low gasp, another *shush*. Janine raised an eyebrow.

So I spoke.

"Hello." There was no response.

"Hello? We... we come in peace." I sighed. What a stupid thing to say, like I was an emissary visiting another planet. Whoever was on the other side of the wall remained quiet. Hank and Janine also tried to get them to speak — "Anyone there?" "We don't mean you any harm" — then relented. Still no response.

I took a deep breath. Then my mouth opened and words came out on their own, without thought. "I know you don't know me, don't know any of us," I said. "And I know you have a good reason not to trust us. But I'm *tired*, I'm *really tired*, and we need your help. So, since I know you're in there, I'm just going to sit down here and tell you my story. The whole thing. Then you can decide what to do."

I plopped down on the floor and rested my back against the locked doors. And for the better part of an hour, I just talked.

* * *

After I was done, we sat there in silence, the three of us, matching the silence we heard on the other side of the doors.

A moment passed and nothing. Then, quietly, a man spoke. "You carry the cure in your blood?" he asked, skepticism mixed with a barely detectable note of greed in his voice.

"Yes," I said, smiling at the sound of this new voice. Janine and Hank were wide-eyed with surprise. I guess none of us actually expected a response of any kind.

There was another long pause. Some muffled words, a debate we couldn't hear.

"You're going to have to prove that," the man finally said.

I sighed. "And just how do you propose I do that?"

The doors moved, just a little, and I jumped up, allowing them to swing free. But they didn't open very far. The doors separated just enough to reveal a man, scraggly grey hair and beard, like a mirror of myself, but wearing glasses and a blue lab coat. With the chains still locking the doors together, preventing them from opening any farther, he held something out to me, through the gap.

A hypodermic syringe.

Beside him, others stood. Four men and a woman. Also in lab coats. The woman looked at me with a deep sort of anger, one I didn't understand. Then one of the men pointed a gun at me, and Hank jumped up. As he reached for his own weapon, the man spoke.

"Stop! Stop now, or this is done. We can close the doors, and you'll never get what you came for." Hank froze.

I stepped up to the doors, just inches from the man on the other side. "Let me guess," I said, starting to roll up one sleeve. "Blood sample?"

He nodded.

In just a couple of minutes, it was done. He left me with a swab of cotton to hold on the tiny puncture wound.

The man looked the three of us over as he stood there, needle pointing toward the ceiling, syringe filled with my dark blood. "Might as well get comfortable. This is going to take a while."

Then the doors shut with a loud click, and he was gone.

21

The light behind the doors came back on, as did the low hum of some sort of machinery. Hours went by. Hank and Janine both seemed nervous, wired. They paced, checked and rechecked their weapons. I slept.

In the still darkness, an untold time later, the doors opened, chains falling away with a clattering sound. I jolted awake and stood, waiting to see what would happen.

And she stepped out.

For a moment, just a moment in my spinning mind, I thought it was Rosa. I swiped at my eyes, rubbing away sleep, then a tear or two. But no, it wasn't her.

The woman, the one in the lab coat who'd first looked at me with such reproach, walked out between the open doors. She stepped in front of me, and without a word did something no one expected.

She hugged me.

* * *

She'd known Rosa. She'd actually known Rosa. They worked together at NIH headquarters before Rosa pushed for her transfer to Capitol Hill.

The woman's name was Phebe Silvos. She'd worked with Rosa for three years in the very same building where we were standing, and she knew Rosa was a good and honest person. She'd heard about Rosa and me on the hill overlooking DC, about Rosa's message and her death, and simply didn't believe any of it. Someone was making up stories of a cure that didn't exist, abusing the name of Rosa, her friend who was missing and who, she'd assumed, had been dead for many months before this all happened.

And now here I was, the other half of that tale, showing up just outside her door. In a rush, Phebe told me how they took my blood and ran tests on it. She said something about analyzing its reaction with preserved zombie blood, and rattled off a bunch of terms and processes that spun even my head. Her laboratory and my experience as a general practitioner were many miles apart.

Phebe let go of me and sobbed, turning back to her colleagues. "You know we need to go," was all she said to them.

One of the men, the one who'd held the pistol on me, and still held it by his side, pointed downward, replied. "No," he said. "No, we don't. They'd *kill* us, if they knew we even thought about it." For a moment, the other men wavered, but not Phebe.

"I don't care," she said. "I'm going."

"I don't understand." I couldn't think of anything else to say.

"The *director*," Phebe said. "He wants a cure, but for himself, for his people, not for everyone else. He won't say so, but we know it. Ever since the story about Rosa, and the revolution, things have been bad. Very, *very* bad. The director pushes us. He says if Rosa could figure it out, why can't we? He left us here, but his people always come back. They'll be back to check on us. *And soon.*" She looked down at her watch, then at us with eyes of desperation.

"Who's the director?" I asked.

"Director McDaniels, the head of NIH. He's really an Army guy, a colonel or something. Not a scientist at all. The military swept in and kicked out all the old guard a long time ago. Right after the outbreak." Phebe shook her head. "He's not a nice guy. We don't want to be here when his people come back."

Janine chimed in. "But we didn't come here just for *you*. What about your machines and your lab?"

"That can't be helped now," Phebe said. "There are other labs. But this one isn't safe." She looked like a fox in a leg trap, wild with the need to get away. "Look, I know my stuff. It'll be hard, especially getting another lab setup, but I can do it. Wait — you have power, right?" I nodded, and she let out a huge sigh of relief. "Then take me with you. Let me try."

The man who had taken my blood suddenly spoke up. "I'll go, too," he said. The other men in lab coats looked shocked.

"But —" one of them cried.

"The director —" another added.

"The director is an evil man, and I've had enough of him," the man said, taking off his glasses and wiping them on the hem of his lab coat. He turned his attention back to us. He'd heard my story, and must have believed it. "This Oasis of yours in Maryland. Annapolis? How long will it take us to get there?"

Hank interrupted. "Hold on. Our people back in DC. We need to get them first."

I shot him a look. *Not now.* "What's your name?" I asked the man with the glasses.

"Joseph," he replied.

"Come on, then, Joseph," I said. "Let's go." Turning to the other men, I asked, "Are any of you coming with us?" They stood frozen as if in ice.

In the end, Joseph and Phebe were joined by two of the other men, Sanjit and Kenshin. The four of them gathered only the supplies they could carry, a few personal items, a few things from the lab. Two other men stayed behind. Phebe teared up as we started to leave. "Will you be safe?" she said them. "What'll you tell McDaniels?" They didn't reply, but just watched us leave.

* * *

There was no way we could make the reverse journey across the divide right away. It was after nightfall as we left the lab building, and

I wasn't the only one unwilling to make the attempt in the dark. The first order of business was to get clear, somewhere we wouldn't be found by either McDaniels' men or whatever random zombies were about. NIH's walls encircled a lot of land, a lot of other buildings. Joseph suggested an abandoned maintenance building on the southeast corner of the campus, and we hastened to get there.

Overnight, as we slept propped against the walls of a grimy room in a grimy building, I heard tiny sobs from the two newcomers. I had no idea what they were leaving behind; they had no idea what was lying ahead.

* * *

In the morning, Hank and Janine faced an unenviable task: get a group of seven people, four of whom had no experience outside the walls, across the divide. Hank shook with nervous energy. Janine looked determined, but her occasional sideways glances at Hank told me she was concerned.

For me, I had a feeling, deep in my gut, that this was the end of the journey. Between the lingering pain of my many injuries, my age, the losses I'd suffered — I just didn't think I could take much more. I was hopeful that I'd found the people we needed. Somehow, the rest would have to take care of itself. Like a wave crashing ashore, I felt I'd gone as far as I could, and now it was time to retreat back to the sea.

Phebe didn't know me, but she was perceptive. She studied me with a strange, careful eye. "Are you all right?" she asked as we prepared to leave.

"Yeah, yeah," I said, waving away her concern. But I wasn't all right. My arm, shoulder, and chest throbbed with old wounds. But more than that, my heart was heavy. "Hank," I said, getting his attention. "When we get back to HQ, the hospital, I want to leave for Annapolis as soon as possible. The same day, if we can. It's time to leave the city behind once and for all." I could tell Hank wasn't sure where this request was coming from. "And besides," I added, lowering my chin, "I have a debt to pay." Visions of Oliver, backing away from the open doorway, filled my mind. *What did Oliver tell them? Celia must think I'm dead. If she's not dead herself.*

I knew there was very little holding Hank in DC. It wasn't his city, not originally. And he wanted something better, for his people, for himself. For Janine.

Hank had heard my entire story. Everyone in our small group had. I didn't bother leaving out Oliver's treachery when I told my tale to the scientists. Now, after a few moments of reflection, Hank seemed to understand that it was about more than the cure. He clapped a hand on my shoulder. "If Oliver hadn't done what he did, I'd probably never have seen you again, or had this chance to help find a cure. So in a weird way, I should thank him." I shuddered at the thought. Hank went on. "But that doesn't excuse him. What he did was unforgiveable. I want to help you repay that debt, any way I can."

So we set off.

* * *

One thing was sure, I was careful. I'd be damned if I was going to fall into that water again.

The four scientists did their best to follow Hank and Janine's lead. In fact, they even helped me, providing a steady hand here and there as we crossed the river. While we saw zombies, they were farther off, and didn't chase us. And Phebe and her colleagues were so new to the outside world that we didn't need to remind them to keep a healthy dose of fear in their hearts. With them, fear might have been all they had.

By the end of the day, we were back inside the more familiar part of the walled city. As we approached the hospital, it felt almost like a letdown. We had escaped the domain of Director McDaniels, crossed the divide, and found our way back to safe haven. And not much happened. I almost wished something had. I felt like there were very bad things waiting out there for Phebe and the others, and I wanted them to be ready. But I kept quiet. A day of peace was worth savoring.

We didn't get within 200 yards of the building before the feeling of calm satisfaction was whisked away.

"Janine, Hank, it's urgent!" It was James, in his faded fatigues, running up to us. They didn't say a word in response. They just ran.

* * *

We'd only left the morning before, but something had gone terribly wrong while we were gone. At some point, a kid — a boy of maybe 10, no parents, taken in by the group — had been bitten, infected, while he was outside the hospital. For whatever reason, he played it off. Maybe foolishness, maybe ignorance, maybe desperation. But he kept it quiet. He hid it. And then, he turned.

He slept in a room with other kids, all orphans of the disease. And during the night we were away, he bit three of them before he could be restrained. The entire group was in a panic, tempers flaring all around.

It wasn't until I walked in trailed by the four scientists in their lab coats that the arguments fell quiet. A woman who spent most of her time caring for the orphans grabbed at my shirt as I brushed past her. *"Do you have it?"* she pleaded. I stammered, noncommittal, and she turned to Phebe, pawing her like a desperate animal. *"Do you?"*

Phebe looked at her, equal parts revulsion and pity, trying to pull away. "It doesn't work that way," she said. "I — *We* have a lot of work to do. It's going to take a lot of time. I'm sorry."

"We don't have a lot of time!" the woman said. They're just kids!" She wailed, but two other women came up and hugged her, consoled her. Reluctantly, she let herself be led away.

We put down the first kid that same day. Within four days' time, we had to put down the other three infected kids, too. After that, it was hard to find anyone who wanted to stay in DC. By the seventh morning, our entire group was standing at the front doors of the old hospital, ready to leave.

22

We gathered in the street before daybreak, hundreds of people. Less than a dozen wanted to stay behind. Then, as they saw the others pack up to leave, they broke down and joined us. No one wanted to be left alone. Or miss out on the cure.

Hank had sent scouts to every other huddled group of people living nearby. No one else chose to join us, even after hearing our story. I can't say I was surprised. Would I believe it if I hadn't lived it?

The light of day was just starting to creep into the eastern sky, a peach-tinted glow. There had been some rain during the night, but it had moved on to the north, and the day was dawning a little warmer than those before it. A thin bank of fog clung to the ground in all directions, not enough to blind us, but lending a mysterious air to the day. Like it was all a dream. Except for the sounds of straps being cinched or the occasional cough, it was quiet. The group was too nervous for idle chatter.

Phebe, Joseph, Sanjit, and Kenshin — who went by Ken — were pressed into the middle of the pack. I didn't come out and say it, but I tried to make sure they had a place of relative safety, deep in the center. We had fought so hard, done so much to find them, we needed them safe.

Hank and Janine filtered through the crowd, ensuring that everyone was set, all the supplies were packed and ready, all the children were supervised, weapons were loaded.

We hadn't even set off before we saw them, the goddamned infected.

At first, they looked more like aimless feral animals, frittering around in the distance, scavenging for any small morsel. I don't think any of them actually saw us. Maybe they heard something. Maybe *felt* something. They were so far away that we couldn't hear a sound. They were just ghostly apparitions, dimly moving in the fog.

A general sense of unease went through the large group. Hank had a decision to make: move or stay. More than one person was eyeing the hospital, considering a quick return to home and safety.

Hank spoke in a loud whisper. "Not everyone can hear me, and we need to be quiet. Once I'm done talking, pass this along to the people behind you, but keep your voices low." He looked around to be sure he had everyone's attention, at least those close enough to hear. Then he started up again with a new vibrancy. "*We are leaving. We have food and water. We have guns and other weapons, and we have plenty of strong hands to protect us as we walk. We have a plan. This journey is never going to be easy. And there's never going to be a day without those... things* —" Hank waved a hand toward the zombies in the distance. "— *unless we make that day. So we're leaving, now. To get to The Oasis and try to remake the future!*"

It was a lot of bravado, but it did the trick. Slowly, people nodded and turned their backs on the hospital. To Janine, Hank said, "Are we all set on the plan?" She nodded, but he continued, for himself as much as for anyone else, it seemed. "You and the A group up front, in the lead. The rest of the scout groups, B through G, on the flanks, and me with Z group in the back." Each group consisted of four scouts — those people who were most familiar with staying safe in unsafe places. The people used to handling weapons. Janine plus four in the front, three groups of four on each side, and Hank plus four in the back. Thirty-four people guarding more than 300, on a journey that would take us until well past nightfall, if we were lucky enough to make it in one day.

"I remember," Janine said. "We're all set."

"All right. Good luck." And Hank turned and started off toward the back of the group.

Janine grabbed his hand and spun him back around, pulling him close and planting a passionate kiss on his lips. It was the only time I ever saw them publicly display affection. The first... and last.

* * *

Three-hundred souls, plus or minus, with dozens of zombies following behind. We made a macabre parade. Humans huddled together, shuffling feet, pulling carts, a loose circle of defenders around us. And slowly, with an eerie steadiness, zombies trailed after us, drawn by the muted sounds of our passing.

It was like they felt the end was coming, too. Like maybe their options were running low, and they had to do something to try to survive. Without a collective intelligence, it was just animal instinct. But still, they followed. Maybe we could have just waited them out, let them die. But we had a lot to lose, too. If they got to us, it wouldn't matter if they were healthy or in their death throes. We would die, and our last chance would die with us. We worked to stay as far ahead of them as we could.

Janine set the pace as fast as the group could manage, and guided us around any obvious areas of trouble. Hank kept close watch on the rear. On occasion, a zombie would pop up suddenly, near one side or the other, and be put down quickly and quietly by a heavy blow from one of the flanking scouts, usually wielding the hammer weapon I'd first seen Hank use. Some of our people uttered little gasps at these attacks, a few of which were dangerously close to our scientists. *Our scientists.* I realized I'd begun to think of them that way, and of the entire group as *our people.* Maybe even *my people.* I wasn't sure what to make of the idea.

Slowly walking east and out of the city, our huddled mass was shadowed by dozens of zombies. Two oddly symmetrical groups. Us, slogging along, looking for safety, and the infected, nearly blind but following their instincts.

I stayed near the rearguard, close to Hank. Janine was far enough ahead that we couldn't see her except for the rare moments when she was positioned uphill from us. Then she'd crest the hill and disappear again. If I happened to catch Hank's eye, he seemed concerned, watchful of Janine, like he knew something bad was about to happen.

It was only about an hour until we reached the eastern wall. The barricade that for so long had kept the city safe now threatened to become a bottleneck. With a horde of zombies so close behind, we couldn't afford to slow down, but there was no clear way through.

Luckily, Hank had planned for this, too.

Janine's A group trotted ahead as soon as the wall was in sight. In a short while, they gave the *all clear* sign. A few minutes after that, they gave a new sign: *This way.* In a dark space under a bridge, part of the wall had fallen away, and that was where we made our escape from the city. Scout groups B and E went through the gap in the wall first, taking up positions to guard people as they came through. They were followed by Janine's team, who again moved to the front, waiting for the rest of the group.

Slowly, the masses narrowed themselves to nearly single-file and pushed through the opening. In the back, our progress dropped to almost zero, and the throng of zombies that had been shadowing us came closer. A sort of electricity began to build in the air. It was clear something was going to happen, and I could see Hank readying himself, so he could handle it with a clear head.

He ordered two of the flanking groups, D and G, to attach themselves to the rearguard, where they formed a curved line, protecting the group. I saw the scientists from NIH pressing forward, trying to gain the gap and get out. Phebe paused, just for a second, and nodded to me as she ducked through the wall. I stayed back, knowing I couldn't really help Hank, but not wanting to abandon him either.

Trying to spare the group, particularly the slower families and children toward the back, Hank took the fight to the zombies. He waved his hands, urging the scouts forward, and they advanced.

Plowing into the masses of zombies, the scouts used blunt objects and long knives to kill them one after another. Initially, it seemed like easy work. But after a time, the frenzy began. Every new zombie that entered the fray was furious and slathering, a mini whirlwind of chaos. Hank's team was smart and effective, but not superhuman. Little by little, they were driven back, toward me, toward the group.

By then, the middle section of the group had passed through the gap and was gone. But more than a hundred people still remained inside the walls, pushing to get free.

From the side streets, new signs of motion. More zombies, coming to investigate the sounds of violence, bolstering the attacking group. Hank was sweating profusely, and his team was wide-eyed and heaving. The smell of dead zombies overwhelmed every breath, like animal carcasses in a slaughterhouse, reeking and spouting gore. Some of the scouts flinched at the blood; they must have figured it was a sure path to infection. Suddenly Hank took a step toward an attacking zombie, slipped in a puddle of slick blood, and fell to the broken pavement. With an oomph, the air rushed out of his lungs, and the zombie prepared to leap at him.

Without conscious thought, I fired.

I hadn't even realized my pistol was in my hand, yet the zombie fell dead. Hank jumped up, avoiding the spray of blood, gave me a dire look, a nod of thanks.

Then he was springing toward me, pulling out his hammer-like tool. At the last moment, he slid to my left, swung his arm in a harsh downward blow. I just had time to flinch and look sideways as his weapon brained an infected dog that was inches from tearing into my leg.

Then Hank was gone, back into the battle.

God, a *dog*. And a brown one, at that. I blinked, and behind my eyes saw fresh red blood splattered on dry yellow corn, Celia on the ground, blood flowing. Addy dead, but not before she'd been lost to the fury of the disease. My heart sank as I opened my eyes again, not sure which was worse: my memories or my reality. Among the approaching mass of human zombies were other forms: dogs. Many more infected dogs. I don't know why, but all of my conviction drained out of me.

It was lost. Hopeless. An impossible task.

Everything was *lost*.

We were the final hope for a cure, and now we'd come to our end.

There was no way these few scouts could prevail. It was only a matter of time, as the last third of our group pushed frantically toward the gap, trying to get through.

People were shrieking, trying to stop the others behind them from pressing too hard, smothering them. I backed up toward the last of the group as Hank's scouts pulled inward. They formed a tight semicircle, firing weapons, slashing with blunt tools.

Just yards away, a growing wall of zombies surged closer. For another moment, they walked in their slow, frittering way, seeking a distinct target. Former humans, former dogs, and now even infected rats and raccoons moved together in an angry, buzzing cloud, nipping at any close target. They tore at each other even as they looked for us. Their bites didn't seem to mean anything to each other, because their leprosy had robbed them of feeling. Instead, they gave the horde a jarring gait. As a group, they had an odd slowness to their approach, like they were building up to something.

Then, finally, they were close enough to truly see us. In an instant, slow pursuit became manic attack. They jumped.

And we knew we couldn't withstand the assault. We were dead.

Suddenly a sound like 50 cannons exploded in my ears, and the zombies fell, many of them at once. Infected humans, spraying gore. Infected dogs, tumbling onto the pavement, their death throes awful to behold. Infected rats and raccoons, practically vaporized out of existence.

I looked around at Hank and his team, saw they were dumbfounded.

Then, as the zombies fell away, we saw them.

People. Regular living humans, like us, joining the fight from our right flank, wiping out the phalanx of zombies.

Through the zombie horde, we could see them, but barely. Men with guns, arranged like a military assault, but wearing the makeshift, patched clothing that told us they were like us: just another pocket of refugees in the city.

"It's Duke's men!" The call came from somewhere to my right, a voice I didn't recognize. People were helping us? Joining us? Maybe they believed our story after all.

I looked again at Hank, slack-jawed, dead-eyed, splatters of blood and dirt on his face and clothes. He looked so much like a zombie himself, filthy and staring. It gave me pause. *Wait. How will they tell us from the zombies?*

I screamed at the people nearest me. "Wave your hands! Up high!" I raised my hands above my head, shook them wildly. People looked at me, confused. But soon, Hank understood and followed suit, and so did the others. We yelled, we waved. And the approaching onslaught dimmed but didn't disappear. Our saviors began to understand who we were — and what we weren't — and they were adjusting their aim.

But it wasn't fast enough.

Something flashed past me to the left, and I whipped my head to follow it, only to see one of the flanking scouts fall dead to the ground. A young man in his twenties. A stray bullet took away everything he'd ever be, or say, or do. I waved my hands, ever more hysterically, yelling, "Stop! We're human! We're *not infected*!"

Just to my right, I heard a wet sound and something like popping bubbles. With knowing dread, I turned to look, saw Hank as he drew a hand up to his neck, then pulled it away. It was covered in blood, which very quickly soaked his clothing, turning everything a dark purplish red.

Hank fell at my feet, the right side of his neck torn out by a passing bullet, his eyes staring up at me in shock and terror. I dropped to my knees, grabbed him, pressed a hand to the wound, trying to stop the flow of blood. I looked into his eyes. This friend who had saved me on more than one occasion. "No," was all I could say. "No." There wasn't enough tissue left for me to work with. There was nothing I could do.

He tried to talk, but no words came, only more bubbling, more gurgling. Horrible sounds. Sounds that, as a doctor, I knew were beyond repair.

Around us, I had the sense that others had approached, made a circle. Many of them held their breath. With only a quick, desperate glance, I saw new faces. The men who had come to our rescue. And who now stood around me in shock at what they had done. Some bowed their heads. Others closed their eyes. Everyone seemed to know they were watching something awful. In just a few minutes, with too much of his blood seeping into the ground, Hank faded from consciousness.

Oh God, I thought. *No.* I knew it was too late. In only a few minutes more, Hank would be gone. *Thank you for all you've done, my friend. I'm sorry it's your time.* I held his hand as it spasmed uncontrollably.

With a wet rasping sound, Hank took his final breath. And I noticed a pair of feet skid to a stop in front of me.

How? Why? Those were my only thoughts at first. *Why are you here? You don't need to see this. How could you have known to come?*

Janine fell with a wail that tore my heart. She grasped at Hank, tearing him from my grip, causing the last of his blood to spill from his neck. His heart had nothing left to give. She held him, rocking like a mother with child, as Hank left this Earth.

23

With the bulk of the zombie horde destroyed, we pushed the rest of our group through the gap. We'd made it outside DC. To me, this was a welcome liberation, a third time leaving a place that I never wanted to see again. But for almost everyone else in our group, I knew this was a fearful trek into the unknown.

Almost unbelievably, Hank and the young scout — I didn't even know his name — were the only two casualties.

Hank. Damn it. I repeated those last few moments, wondering if there was something I could have done.

Janine walked like a ghost. I'd been next to her as she watched Hank die. Yet that paled in comparison to watching her walk away from his body as we prepared for our final exodus. She left him lying in the middle of the road, hands folded across his chest. A peaceful repose to last eternity. Once Janine turned her head to walk east again, she didn't look back. Her eyes were empty. Her feet moved her along, and she became a painful echo of me in the days and weeks after Rosa died. Janine walked the same way I had, not all that long ago. I knew her soul, knew that she herself didn't understand how she kept going, knew that her mind couldn't even consider the question, knew that she would walk all day and feel no bodily pain. Knew that nothing would cut through the anguish that filled her heart.

The group moved on, with Janine simply occupying a random place in the middle, the people on either side of her guiding her gently along. In her state, there was no point even asking if she'd rejoin the vanguard. The new people, those who'd saved us and accidentally killed Hank, bolstered our surrounding guards, many of them walking with a visibly heavy feeling of guilt. There were about 40 of them, all men, pretty heavily armed, with lot of pistols and ammo. I met their leader, the one named Duke, graying, bearded. He took over the rearguard. But there was a need in the group for some sort of guide to take Janine's place.

That fell to me.

Although the route was simple — back along Route 50 east, straight toward Annapolis — we had to navigate the abandoned cars and dead bodies and cracked pavement that had made long-distance travel since the outbreak so risky. With the others' help, I did my best to steer around anything that looked dangerous and continue forward. But I kept scanning behind, as far back behind our group as I could see, any chance I got.

Most of the zombies following us had been killed in the fray, but not all.

In time, their numbers grew again.

24

With the new people, we were nearly 400 strong. They added significantly to our protective outer ring, but we kept drawing unwanted attention. We were too big of a group to go unnoticed.

I looked back each time I heard some little shout of surprise or the sounds of a scuffle. From time to time, zombies came at us from the sides as we passed. But mostly they just fell in with the ever-growing collection of infected humans, rats, raccoons, and dogs that trailed behind us. They were a good distance off now, but our path was simple to follow — the wide highway. Empty and wrecked vehicles helped shield us from their poor vision, but also slowed our progress. Our inadvertent noise, and maybe just our heat, drew the zombies along. They *sensed* us.

Hours wore on, and miles dropped behind us. I estimated we'd left at around five in the morning. With our size and slow, plodding gait, I thought we'd be lucky to get to The Oasis much before midnight.

In the afternoon, as we walked, I started to think about our biggest problem. *How were we going to get rid of the zombies before we reached Annapolis?* We couldn't just bring them back with us.

I knew our scouts each had at least one pistol and as much ammo as they could carry. They also had their blunt instruments, hammers, axes. One scout, Terrence, from Z group, mentioned to me he had two flare guns and several flares. I considered what to do with that information, but didn't have any great ideas.

I left a scout to lead the way briefly as I faded to the back and talked to Duke. He spoke in a gruff voice, a low bass with a thick, gravelly rasp. From the way his men looked at him, it was clear he led them as more of a father figure than a military general. I immediately liked that about him. He told me that his men had been keeping tabs on our group at the hospital for months. When our scouts had asked them to join us, they were understandably skeptical. But then, when he got the report that we were all headed east, he knew we were leaving, probably for good. He knew about the radio broadcasts, the stories and rumors of a new Oasis. He figured there must be some truth to it if we all were going, and brought his small army to see what was happening. That's when they'd found us and joined the fight.

Duke was a good leader, better by far than me. He'd even had the sense to run two pairs of scouts up ahead on the highway, to look out for approaching trouble or at least identify the best path forward. The scouts alternated coming back at regular intervals to report whatever information they had.

"Duke," I said in a tired voice "We've got to get rid of those things." I nodded behind us at the zombies. "Sooner rather than later."

Duke considered this. He pulled out a package of cigarettes. Tobacco and paper with a synthetic filter, old-school Camels, from before the infection. I couldn't imagine how stale they must have been, but if that was his pleasure, so be it. Now I knew where his rasp came from. He lit a cigarette with a match from a small pack. In that moment, two things occurred to me. First, how smoking had been so common in the old days, even though it was clearly bad for you. Obviously, that was from my past life as a doctor, intruding on my present. Then, from a more current perspective, I thought of how much of an extravagance this was, wasting matches for one man's personal pleasure. I shook off both thoughts as irrelevant to our current situation.

Duke exhaled a plume of blue-gray smoke. "Light. Noise," he said. "That's pretty much it."

"That's pretty much what?" I asked.

"Pretty much all they respond to," he said, puffing little clouds into the crisp spring air.

Of course, I thought. *I knew that.*

I stepped away from him, considering our options. As we gained the top of a small hill, I looked back, seeing ever more zombies staggering after our tired group. We walked on, lost in thought.

Celia, you're like a daughter to me. I love you, and good luck, I thought. I hope you can see through Oliver, at least better than I did.

Celia. And even Janine. They were my hope. A tired smile spread across my face as I walked east, focusing on one idea.

Not much farther.

25

The group was beyond exhausted, our pace slowing miserably. Behind a white wall of clouds, the sun went down, and night came. Thankfully, the moon was nearly full, and cast a bright but muted glow behind the clouds. It was the only light as we walked on and on. Nondescript places passed and faded behind us. I knew we were close to Annapolis.

I was tired. So tired. My many aches, which had started as dull throbs during the day, had grown into deep, unyielding pains. My arm. Shoulder. Leg. Chest. The pieced-together shell of my mortal coil throbbed. I was simply spent. And worse than the physical toll of the journey, Janine's plight brought to mind Rosa, Harvey and The Oasis, even Addy. The dog who hadn't deserved her fate. Still, I was the leader, or one of them. I had to keep going. I twirled the tattered bracelet I wore, barely held together by threads, my only physical connection to Rosa.

The gap between our group and the horde behind us was becoming dangerously narrow. If we couldn't gain some ground, by increasing our speed or delaying the zombies, we'd soon be in the middle of another deadly battle. Duke instinctively saw this and sent some of his men toward the back. He thought a fight was inevitable. I didn't quite agree.

I knew there was another option.

I conferred with Duke, explained my plan, and he nodded, grimly. He sent word through his men, making preparations. They hardly knew me, they had no reason to argue.

But Janine.

I thought she was too far gone to pay attention to what was happening. I thought word could be sent around without breaking her frozen facade. I was wrong.

She snapped to life, like an alarm clock had brought her sleeping body back to consciousness. She rushed right over to me. "What're you doing?" she asked, wild with sudden energy. I looked at her eyes and saw they were bloodshot and raw. She was frayed, like cloth where the seams were pulling apart with age. Or wear.

"I'll do it," she said, and we both stopped walking, even knowing how precious each footstep was, keeping us ahead of the horde. Others slowed around us.

"No, Janine."

"Yes. I have to."

"No," I said again. But what argument did I have? If I invoked Hank's memory, she'd never relent. And while she'd known, Rosa, the pain that was currently overwhelming her wouldn't allow that sort of connection to the past.

In the end, I didn't say anything. Our eyes locked, hands intertwined, and we looked at each other, two souls 40 years different in age. But inside our gaze, there was *understanding*. I believe she knew then that we'd experienced the same thing, and that I had to do this one thing or I'd never find peace. As her tears began to flow, she nodded. But she couldn't let go of my hands, and instead she pulled me toward her, hugging me. Her body shook as she sobbed, and I tried to console her, but a clarity came over me at the same time, and I gently nudged her to start walking again.

* * *

In the full of dark, a pair of Duke's scouts returned again. *We've got to be close*, I thought. Duke talked with the men, then walked over to me as they ran off again. "We've got a bit of a problem," he said.

Just ahead of us was the Severn River bridge. The small arch that had goaded us to turn south and find this new Oasis in the first place. We'd come so far. From the bridge, we'd soon be able to see the three radio towers of our waiting home.

But...

The scouts, mostly looking for zombies to kill or avoid, hadn't expected to find *humans*. In fact, they'd run smack into another group of scouts, moving in the opposite direction, toward us. Scouts from The Oasis. After a moment of contact, they scrambled back to us as the other scouts retreated the way they'd come.

A short time later, a second pair of Duke's scouts made their return trip. They told us about a blockade being erected on the bridge. *Damn it*, I thought. *It has to be Oliver.*

An internal rage flared. I hoped beyond hope that Celia hadn't been swayed by Oliver. There had been two factions at The Oasis when I left, north and south. I wondered which one was in power now.

Before we'd set out from DC, I'd seen someone shoving a bullhorn into a backpack. I asked around, found out where it was, and sent for it. Once I had that in my hand, I pressed hard, urging everyone through the final distance to the bridge.

* * *

"*Oliver!*" I shouted through the bullhorn. "Let us pass!"

I hadn't known for sure that the blockade was Oliver's doing, or even if he'd made it back to The Oasis. But my fears were confirmed when a squat shadow stood up, balancing on the uneven crest of the barricade. Surprisingly, the coward had come himself, and he shouted a reply. "No! We don't have the resources to support you. You've got to find some other place. My men are prepared to shoot if they need to." In the dull moonlight, I couldn't see anything except dark shapes moving on the bridge.

We didn't have time for this game. The zombies behind us would be upon us soon.

"We have the right people now — scientists who can take my blood and make a cure for everyone," I said. "You've got to let us through." I took a long pause, drawing breath. "There are zombies right behind us. If you don't let us in, they won't only be the end of us. They'll be the end of you and everyone at The Oasis." I could hear muted words of concern passing among the men on the bridge with Oliver. I'm sure I knew most of them. Oliver was a cancer, and they had been infected by him. But that didn't make them bad themselves. "Will you really stand by and watch your only hope for a cure destroyed in front of your very eyes?" More murmurs, louder.

I looked back, over the heads of our group. A dark, indistinct mass was heading toward us.

The infected were too close now. I had to decide.

There was no answer from Oliver. I dropped back, grabbed a bag of supplies that Duke had gathered for me. It was very light. Would it be enough? Janine came over, asking again, with her eyes. I shook my head, and she began to cry. She gave me another long hug that threatened to crush my resolve. Just when I thought I'd drop my head to her shoulder and weep, she pulled away, and in a moment I was sure of myself again. I had to go. We exchanged nods, and I stepped away.

I jogged to the back of the group, where the scouts were directing people toward the others up front. Now that we couldn't go any farther, we were bunching up on the western side of the bridge. I reached into my bag, pulled out the orange plastic form of a flare gun, and popped in a flare. The zombies were close enough that I could hear their ragged march, see individual shapes emerging from the night.

I called out to the group. "Everyone stay down and stay quiet!" My shouting drew the keen attention of the zombies. Their pace quickened. It was time.

I swiveled to my right, aimed the flare gun at a bank of trees just beside the highway, and fired.

The flare blazed hot, a tiny sun of bright red, illuminating the night. Just before it hit the trees, I heard a commotion from the bridge. I almost turned to see what was happening, but then the world exploded as the flare hit a tree and bounced down into the overgrowth. It hissed and burned in the long grass, and the nearest zombies devolved into frenzy, rushing toward it. The flare didn't last long, but it was enough to ignite some of the grass. Zombies dove toward the heat and light, at first frantic to reach the source, then, when they started to burn, frantic to get away. But the other zombies piling up behind them made their escape impossible.

We watched as a pocket of zombies — human, dog, rat, raccoon — collapsed into the fire and were consumed, flailing in terror and pain.

But it wasn't enough.

The zombies that were too far away to be compelled into the blaze continued to walk toward us.

All of my options had been exhausted. With a heavy sigh, I lifted the bag, ran toward the fire.

Behind me, I heard Janine gasp.

Nearing the blaze, I ran through a break in the tall barrier wall that skirted the highway, and dove into the woods. A few zombies followed, but not the bulk of the group.

I pulled out the bullhorn. "Hey! Hey! Here!" I screamed. "*Come to me! Come on, you bastards!*" I made senseless sounds, just to keep up the noise, just to get their attention.

Slowly, the mob turned.

As I backed into the trees, away from every living human I knew, I fired a second flare, off to my right. Another bouncing, blazing comet in the dark night. The two fiery red beacons, along with my wordless ranting on the bullhorn, continued to turn the zombies toward me. The ones in front were chasing me directly. Those behind simply mimicked the ones they followed.

For a moment, I stared.

One man. A dark copse of trees and who knew what beyond. A hundred infected creatures, maybe more. For a second, my heart sank with hopelessness. Then something happened.

I reached the very bottom of despair, with nowhere farther to fall.

And my heart turned to stone.

Through the bullhorn, I shouted, "Come and get me, you sons of bitches!" I laughed, made whooping calls, turned and pushed into the trees. I fired a third flare, making a trio of growing blazes. Zombies walked into them and were burned. But others kept after me.

I staggered and fell, nearly tumbling down a small hill. The moon offered only the slightest visibility amid the trees, and the three fires behind me only deepened the crazily shifting shadows as I ran.

I felt an intense ache, deep, deep inside.

An ache not directly connected to any of my injuries, but an ache in my soul. A weariness of *being*.

It made me even more angry.

Spinning around, I saw two infected dogs closing on me, and I popped in another flare, fired. The red flame zipped along the closest dog's knobby backbone and set its fur alight. The dog howled, and with a mindless fury, the other dog dove at him, tearing into him before sensing the flames that quickly spread to his own body.

I had two flares left.

I continued down the incline, and my foot splashed into water. Immediately, I stopped and turned my head.

In the pale moonlight I could see that I'd exited the tree line and reached the edge of the river. I had to either change course, swim, or be overtaken by the diseased creatures chasing after me. The water was still frigid, with summer a month or more away. I decided to change course.

And a beacon called to me.

A white beast, almost glowing in the light of the moon, in stark contrast to the black waters and shadowed woods around it.

A sailboat.

I raced along the curve of the shore, toward a small dock that jutted into the river. Behind me, shouts and frenzy followed, but I didn't want the zombies to give up on me. I fired another flare into the woods, lighting another glowing blaze. And again I shouted wordless insults into the bullhorn. *Just follow me, you bastards. For the love of God, follow me.*

In droves, they did. I saw so many shapes rushing out of the woods, through the manic red flames and dancing shadows, toward me. Large and small, they came toward the lights and the blaring sound. I found a button on the bullhorn that set off a shrieking alarm, and held it down. It drove them even more mad.

I stumbled through the irregular scrub of the shoreline, over to the dock. What I planned to do once I reached the boat, I had no idea. But it was a goal, any sort of goal.

Behind me, snaps and growls. Several zombies pitched into the muddy water and couldn't get out. They flailed and raged as the waters took them. The others followed my sound, my high, piercing beacon.

I felt the accumulated anger of their numbers, and I threw it back at them. *I hate you all, forever.* It wasn't a rational thought, but I was beyond rational thought. The disease had taken everything from me, my former life, my job, my love, my friends, my health. And now, there was nothing standing between me and the infected. I jumped onto the dock.

With a *flap flap flap* I pounded along the warped planks, eyeing the boat, hoping it would offer some shelter. I stepped over the railing, the frayed and useless cable, and onto the deck. Carefully maneuvering toward the cockpit, I ducked in and out of the vertical wires that held the mast tense and upright. I spared a glance back to see several dozen zombies spilling onto the dock. *Shit*, I thought. *Shit, there's no time at all.*

I fumbled for the wooden slats that barred entry to the cabin, saw a tiny padlock securing them shut. I dropped the bullhorn, still blaring its alarm, onto the floor of the cockpit.

Without thinking, I slammed the hard plastic flare gun into the small metal lock, and the lock burst open. My hand caught on the clasp and the skin tore, blood speckling the boat's white frame.

A tall, ropy zombie leaped onto the boat, landing right next to me, but I'd already loaded the last flare. As he moved to strike me, I fired, and red flames erupted in his gut. He screamed a hideous scream, burning alive. I dove for the hatch.

And I felt it tear away. Time froze as that multi-colored bracelet she had made for me fell. Rosa's bracelet. A worthless trinket, invaluable. It dropped toward the edge of the boat. Before I could move, it slipped off the side of the boat and into the waiting waters below.

There was no time left, but I spared a moment anyway. A moment to remember. To weep. To steel myself. And to be reborn.

My rage became infinite.

With pure fury, I pushed back the hatch and started to pull out the first of the wooden slats, but another zombie fell into the cockpit, drawn to me and to the infected man still burning behind me. I took two instinctive steps up toward the open hatch, ducking to miss the boom. It was irrational, but rational thought had left me.

I dropped inside.

* * *

Pain hit me everywhere, as I collided with the steep wooden stairs, tumbled, and fell into the cabin. My head hit the side of a bench and I ended up on my back, stunned, staring up through the open hatch at the uncaring night sky above.

I heard a thud.

Then another, and another. Steps. Snarls and snaps. The zombie I'd hit with the flare kept blazing in the rear of the cockpit. Others jumped or fell into the boat and immediately went to him, drawn by the flames and the harsh sound of the bullhorn. They were burned as they approached. It kept repeating. Zombies fell into the flames, roared their pain. More thuds on the deck, more frantic steps, more shrieks.

And...

The boat...

Was it dipping lower in the water? How many zombies had jumped on board?

I was still on my back, looking up at the sky, and for a moment the clouds parted and a single star shone down on me.

Damn you, I thought. *Damn you.*

The single star mocked me. Aloof, distant, uncaring. Nothing that I'd ever done, ever loved, ever wanted, mattered to that star, not one bit.

I had nothing left but rage.

The bracelet, my last real connection to her, was gone.

I struggled to my feet, just as one of the infected bastards — his slashed and pitted face framed by long, stringy hair — popped into view, peering blindly down through the hatch. I started, but then my anger grew even greater. I reached up and grabbed the hatch. And as the zombie extended its spindly arms down toward me, I slammed the hatch home, breaking bones.

Even with its diminished ability to feel, the thing let out a horrible cry. I relented long enough to let it pull back its broken limbs. Then I closed the hatch completely.

26

On deck, sound and fury reigned. The deafening bullhorn, the burning zombie, the zombie shrieking with broken arms, and countless others drawn to the noise and light. The boat was definitely dipping lower in the water.

More thuds and snarls. More zombies on the boat. And splashes, and the frantic sounds of survival. Zombies were drowning. *How many had I killed? How many were left?*

I stumbled through the dark cabin, toward the south-facing portholes. I needed to see what was happening.

Outside, in the dull glow of moonlight obscured by clouds, I saw a throng of infected on the dock, just feet away, pressing against the boat. As I watched, some leaped over onto the deck, some fell into the dark waters, and some stayed put, raging on the pier. Behind them, past the dock, I saw it. The bridge.

Up on top were the forms of several people, some sort of standoff.

Could it be? That short, stubby figure… Oliver? And another person, taller, thinner. I wanted to believe it was Celia. In an instant, my heart realized how much I'd missed her.

The short one was being cowed, pushed back, losing position. The taller one was taking control. I wished I could hear what was being said, understand what was happening.

Then, a mass of movement. Dozens of people, hundreds, rushing across the bridge. From my right, heading to my left, toward the east. Toward The Oasis.

It had to be Celia. She'd wrested control from Oliver. The bridge was finally clear, and the people from DC were getting through. They let out a huge cheer.

A very, very *loud* cheer.

No.

Don't.

Closer to me, I saw the first reactions. Zombies turned their heads. Away from the mayhem on the boat, and back toward the bridge.

No...

I pressed one palm against the porthole's glass, willing them to stop.

The horde, though diminished from losing so many members to fire and water, was still formidable.

And suddenly, incomprehensibly, they were turning away from me.

* * *

For what seemed like eternity, I sat in the cabin, on the raised seat, looking through the porthole. Watching them leave. To attack my friends again. And I knew what the zombies would find. At the back of the group were the slow ones: the women with children, the elderly, the infirm. Involuntarily, I let a moan escape, a sound of remorse.

What more can I do?

I slammed a fist sideways into the leg of the chart table, then immediately regretted it. My hand throbbed, seemingly in time with all my other injuries. The table leg cracked and buckled, and the table's top slid partly open.

I closed my eyes.

This is the end...

This is the end...

My eyes popped back open.

The end? Of what? Of the world? Hardly. It will endure. Of humanity? Probably not. People still lived in random pockets here and there. Of The Oasis and the cure? That was it. That was what I couldn't bear. Rosa had led me to this path, and I couldn't let it go. I couldn't let her go before every ounce of my strength was gone, too.

I slammed my other fist into the table, to hell with the pain.

My mind went back to the one thing that I could never erase from my vision: Rosa's death. Her head snapping back, over and over again. I shook my head, squinted my eyes.

I don't want this!

I screamed at the heavens. I screamed it, again and again, spittle flying.

I don't want this!

My heart felt like it would burst from anger, rage, fear, loneliness, longing, hate. Love.

And there, in the open crack of the chart desktop, was an answer.

A tinge of orange plastic.

27

I've made up my mind.

I hope they have enough, with Celia and Janine and all the researchers. But there's nothing more I can do.

Except save them. Give them a chance to write their part of this horrible tale. I'll pull every one of these damned infected bastards toward *me* and away from *them*.

I'm going to go out.

I've gathered the new orange flare gun from the chart table. There were even six flares. I popped in the first, and have the others in my pocket. Maybe they'll all work, or maybe not.

Maybe I'll make it 10 steps. Or maybe not.

But I'm going to do it and I'm going to keep on firing.

Until I can't do it anymore.

For Celia and the others, and the researchers of the new Oasis. God, I hope you can do it. *Please.*

For Harvey, Hank, and Janine of the old Oasis. May your legacy lead to the cure.

For Rosa.

For Rosa.

Without you, the world would never have even had a chance. Nor would I.

I love you.

Maybe I'll see you soon.

I'm going out to raise hell among the damned now.

EPILOGUE

If you're reading this, you need to know.

He saved them. Those hundreds of people on the bridge. Every one. He gave himself up for them, the people he barely knew.

I found these pages four months ago, in the boat he hid in, still tied to the dock. I don't really know how to write this, but I feel I need to add something. To fill in something at the end. To put something down for whoever comes next. Because you need to know. If he hadn't done what he did, they probably all would have died.

And if we're the last, or the seed for whatever is next, he made it happen. He took the zombies away. He gave himself up.

We saw him, at the last, overwhelmed by the horde. He was my friend and I will always miss him. Without him, I would have been dead a long, long time ago.

He was a doctor, in the truest sense. He healed people. I mean, in the end, he might have even healed the world. His blood is in us all now. Through me.

They got it to work, the researchers from NIH. It was hard as hell, and took a very long time. But they built a new lab, got equipment. And they used my blood and Janine's blood to find the cure. To replicate it.

We've been able to cure almost every person who has come to us. A few people get sick and die, and that hits us all hard, since we're trying to save them. But for the most part, they all live.

At last count, there are more than two thousand of us. We've annexed the peninsulas on either side of the new Oasis. We have teams cleaning up the nearest parts of Annapolis, and there are many among us who plan to relocate there soon.

We've taken down the fences. We're free again. There are still zombies — humans, dogs, rats, raccoons… we even found infected cats and mice — but since we're now cured, we deal with them differently. We know they're lost, and that they have to be put down.

But the total fear is gone. They can hurt us, they can kill us if we aren't careful. But they can't *infect* us. And one day, we hope, we will outlast them.

Our children can live free. Our people can sleep soundly. The zombies live on, for now. But they can't win.

As I write this, it's been 12 months since they began distributing the cure. The first year of freedom has passed, the first year of freedom in too long.

Every day I think of the blood in my veins, the blood that saved me and so many others. His blood. I know his whole story now, from these pages. I know that most people would have given up.

The word goes out and the people come in, every day now. *Look for the three towers. Come to us for the cure. Come to The Oasis.*

And even though he isn't here, it's *his* Oasis. His legacy, in honor of Rosa, and a gift to us all.

We are all his children.

> —   Celia Frederick
>   The Free City of Oasis, Maryland
>   Year 1

THE END

Thank you so much for reading my book! Here's a little bit about me, Keith Soares. I live in Alexandria, Virginia, with my wife and two daughters. By day, my wife and I run a web, mobile and app development studio, which means that writing is my second job. Creativity has always been a huge focus for me, whether making music, coding video games, drawing or writing. *The Oasis of Filth* is my first published novel.

Visit my website at **http://keithsoares.com** for information on other books and upcoming projects. While you're there, I hope you consider joining my mailing list where I can keep you updated on future books.

www.ingramcontent.com/pod-product-compliance
Lightning Source LLC
Chambersburg PA
CBHW030924120626
46554CB00001B/267